Theirs to Protect

by

Melissa Klein

This is a work of fiction. Names, characters, places, and incidents are either the product of the author's imagination or are used fictitiously, and any resemblance to actual persons living or dead, business establishments, events, or locales, is entirely coincidental.

Theirs to Protect

Contact Information: info@thewildrosepress.com

Cover Art by *Angela Anderson*

The Wild Rose Press, Inc.
PO Box 708
Adams Basin, NY 14410-0708

Visit us at www.thewilderroses.com

Publishing History
First Scarlet Rose Edition, 2016
Print ISBN 978-1-5092-1226-2
Digital ISBN 978-1-5092-1227-9

Published in the United States of America

Can Claire keep her hardwired-to-rescue guys from discovering her secret, or will her past send her running again?

"I want to veg out in front of the television," she said. *Sandwiched between you two.* They hung out eating pizza and watching movies at least once a week since she moved in with them. It was one of the things she'd miss most when she moved on.

"Only if Sean or I get to pick." Max used the hand that had been resting on her shoulder to mess up her hair. "Isn't that right?" He punched his buddy in the shoulder. "I declare tonight a no chick-flick movie night."

"Whatever Claire wants." Sean scrubbed a palm over his face. "After last shift, EMT school today, and then having to dress up like an idiot for the calendar, I'm beat." Frown lines furrowed his normally happy face. Even as he'd been coaxing her into spending Christmas with his family, she sensed his mind had been on something else.

Her two friends couldn't be more different. Where Sean was sweet, patient, and easy to talk to, Max had this whole strong, silent thing going for him when he wasn't ripping into someone with his wit. Her gaze darted between the two as they traded good-natured barbs. She couldn't stay in the dark place the package and letter from her hometown had put her in. Not when he was determined to make her laugh, and Max was heating her body to the boiling point.

Dedication

To Eric, the inspiration for all my heroes

Chapter One

Claire Matthews stomped the snow off her boots before heading inside Gun 'N' Hoses, the bar she and her roommates frequented. If she was still in town come February or March, she might be singing a different tune, but for now the girl from Alabama couldn't help thinking the huge flakes made it seem more like Christmas as they swirled in the wind and caught in her hair.

Her hand slipped into the pocket of her parka, grasping the letter from Townsend County Superior Court. Her stomach knotted knowing it might signal it was time for her to move on, despite having put down roots in Chicago. She had two semesters at Northwestern under her belt and a job she didn't totally hate, even if she had been nearly trampled by crazed shoppers two weeks earlier on Black Friday.

She paused in the doorway of the bar's back room taking in the dozen cops and firefighters recruited to pose for a fundraiser calendar. Despite the abundance of bare-chested men, only her two roommates interested her—far more than she was willing to admit. Sean Dalton posed in front of a cardboard fireplace, a pair of short-skirted "elves" flanking either side. Stripped to the waist of his bunker gear and wearing a red and white felt hat, Mr. December likely made every girl there want to start a fire someplace. His heart was as big as his biceps. Besides posing for the calendar, which would raise money for Safe House, a residential facility for homeless women and children, he worked in the shelter's kitchen on his days off.

Claire met him and his best friend, Max Devon, six months ago when she answered their ad for a roommate on the bulletin board in Northwestern's student union. Her attraction to both the men had been growing ever since. Unable to choose between them, she'd kept her feelings under wraps. Now, it seemed as if fate had yanked that decision away from her.

While she'd been fixated on one, she hadn't seen the other approaching. Max Devon wrapped a thick arm around her, pulling her in for a kiss. This wasn't any friendly peck on the cheek either. His mouth moved against hers, warming her from her lips which were answering his demand to open and let him plunder deeper, to her toes curling inside her boots. When he finally broke the kiss after several seconds, she blinked up at him.

"Mistletoe," he answered, holding a sprig over her head. Then he shot her one of his trademark bad-boy grins. At six-three and with dark hair and chocolate eyes everything about him screamed trouble, right down to the sinful things he did to a pair of jeans and biker jacket. Tonight he wore his policeman's uniform, which he filled out very nicely and made her wonder what it would be like get a good frisking from him. He, too, put in off-hours caring for the community he'd sworn to protect and serve by mentoring a group of middle school boys.

With an arm still around her, his brows furrowed. "You got off work over an hour ago. Where you been?"

Sometimes his overly protective ways got on her nerves. After all, she'd been taking care of herself for the past five years. Life was about to get a whole lot more treacherous, so tonight it felt good to have someone give a crap what happened to her. "Christmas shopping." She patted the large bag on her shoulder.

After finishing her shift at the department store, she took the crosstown bus to her post office box. Anyone from her past needing to contact her sent things there. Along with the letter, she found a package from her family which she stowed in her bag underneath the wallet she purchased for Max and Sean's tie.

"Come watch?" He tugged on her arm.

Claire's gaze shot back to the other room. One of the "elves" traced her hands over Sean's chest then stood on tiptoe to whisper something in his ear. He turned the color of the trim on his hat while jealousy churned in her stomach. She could hardly blame the busty redhead for trying. Those full lips of his could do some serious damage to a girl's skin. Not that she was going to get the opportunity to find out.

She watched to see if he would take the girl up on her offer. He did sometimes. Between him and Max, mornings were often a guessing game as to whom she'd find in the kitchen they shared in their Lincoln Park house. There was even that one time when she overheard her roommates as they shared a woman.

"No thanks. I want to get off my feet for a while." Sure, her dogs were barking after eight hours standing in her high-heeled boots, but she also needed to wrap her head around the effects the letter brought to her life. With Billy Townsend out of Evergreen Psychiatric Hospital, it was inevitable he'd come looking for her again. His oath was the last thing he said before the Townsend county deputies hauled him out of the courtroom—that and calling her a lying bitch.

"Suit yourself," Max said, giving her cheek a kiss. Her gaze trailed after him as he walked away. He no sooner stepped inside the room than a blonde dressed in a skintight snowsuit moved in on him. *Siren Sharks.* That's what Claire called the women who prowled around the cops and firefighters who hung out at the bar. It seemed there'd been no shortage of women willing to volunteer to pose with Chicago's finest and hottest.

When Max's shot finished, he moved to stand next to his best friend. Sean's head turned from the woman who was still rubbing against him to say something to Max. Perhaps another three-way was in the works. Claire would gladly trade the purse she bought as a present for herself in exchange for a chance to be the girl-filling between those two.

****

Sean knew the minute Claire entered the bar. Even across the room, she lit him up like someone attached a strand of Christmas lights to his thumbs. He'd been crushing hard on his roommate ever since he laid eyes on her back in the summer.

At first, he tried talking Max out of choosing her as a tenant. They had several people call about the ad and going by the hard-on he got during her interview, seeing her parade around their living room in her panties would make studying for his paramedic certification even more difficult than it already was. After reminding him how much they needed help on the mortgage, Max also said Claire didn't seem the type to

4

flaunt her body.

They were both right. Except for one time when he caught her coming out of the bathroom wrapped only in a towel, he'd never seen her when she wasn't wearing the oversized clothes she favored. It didn't matter what she wore. Sean spent more time fantasizing about her than was good for his chances at becoming an EMT, though that was certainly no fault of hers.

His temper burned, watching Max kiss their girl.

Roommate. Whatever.

He thought about making a move on her, and not in the way Max was. Sean wanted to take her in his arms and kiss her until she melted those soft curves into his body. Then he'd make love to her until she agreed to be his girlfriend. He watched her hungrily as she settled into the booth and pulled a piece of paper out of her coat pocket.

"My place is just around the corner," Santa's Helper whispered in his ear. She was pretty enough if you liked the Botoxed look, or wanted a meaningless fuck—which he sometimes did. Lately, casual hookups weren't what they once were. Max approached, and now he had an easy escape from the girl who was rubbing circles over his pecs as if she was greasing him up like a Christmas goose.

"I bet that makes it very convenient for you," he said stepping away. "If you'll excuse me, my buddy and I need to talk."

The two moved out of the way of the next set of calendar volunteers. "Claire's finally here," Max said, shooting a thumb over his shoulder.

Sean clenched his fist. "I saw her." Good thing they'd had been best friends since high school.

Otherwise, he might forget he needed his hands for work and not punching that shit-eating grin off the guy's face. "I also saw what you did."

Max shrugged. "Not like you're making a move on her."

His temper spiked, despite realizing Max was goading him into doing something about his attraction to the petite brunette. "Don't you think hooking up with a roommate is a bad idea?" That wasn't his only reason. The three of them had an easy-going relationship, and he was afraid to mess things up.

"I don't know," Max said, his grin slipping into a smirk. "Let me try it out, and I'll tell you."

Sean rolled his eyes at his friend's idea of a joke. The guy was very protective of Claire, checking up on her and running off guys at the bar he didn't think were good enough for her. But maybe he was only half kidding about hooking up with her. "I'm going to see if she'll finally tell me what she wants for Christmas."

****

Max watched Sean head over to Claire, wondering if he'd finally get off the stick and do something about his infatuation with their roomie. Seeing her standing in the doorway looking girl-next-door hot inspired him to give his buddy a shove in the right direction. What started as an impulse might be coming back to bite Max in the ass. He was still hard as a telephone pole, and he barely used any tongue when he kissed her.

"Got any more of that mistletoe?" asked the girl who'd been all over Sean a few minutes ago.

She was his usual type: long hair, leggy, and not looking for anything more than a hit-and-run. He looked her over from her double Ds to her eyes, which were bright blue, thickly lined in black, and as cold as the center of his chest. "Sorry, sweetheart. Maybe some other time."

Watching Sean and Claire as they talked warmed something inside him. If he were any kind of upstanding guy, he'd leave the two of them alone. But his best friend's easy humor and her sweet smile drew him in. It wasn't often he let himself get emotionally attached to folks. He learned early in life people had a way of letting you down. Then after his last relationship went into the shitter, he vowed to steer clear of any romantic entanglements.

All that aside, he couldn't stay away. Max headed to the bar to order some drinks for the three of them. "Two beers and a diet cola," he told the bartender, noting the green and red garland draped across the rows of glass bottles.

He thanked his lucky stars the folks organizing the calendar hadn't asked him to play Santa. *God, he hated Christmas*. Not only was crime up during the holidays, and the wind whipping off Lake Michigan a bitch and a half, it reminded him of all the things that were missing from his life.

"I get off in half an hour," the bartender said.

He smiled at the cute blonde as she leaned across the counter, showing off her assets. "Maybe some other time," he said, taking the drinks from her.

She shrugged, in a way that let him know she probably made the offer to others. "That'll be thirteen-fifty," she said before moving away to fill another order.

After paying, Max eased through the crowd to the table where Claire and Sean were sitting. "Here you go, sweetness. I got your usual."

She looked up through a fringe of dark lashes and smiled. "Thanks." She took a sip, holding his attention as he passed one of the beers over to Sean. Her tongue darted out to catch a drop of cola that escaped her plump lips. Max clenched his eyelids, but it was too late. His cock hardened further, making it more than a little painful as he took a seat to her left.

Sean took the beer and after taking a pull on the bottle said, "Tell Claire she needs to come with us to the holiday party my parents are throwing for Safe House this weekend."

He nodded. "Absolutely. Mrs. Dalton really knows how to throw a shindig."

She was also the closest thing he ever had to a real mother. God only knew what would have happened to him if Sean's mom hadn't stepped in when he was a kid. It was for damn sure he'd have never had a square meal or graduated high school. He'd have probably ended up on the other side of the jail cell instead of well on his way to making sergeant.

Claire ran her finger around the rim of her glass. "I don't know. I don't want to intrude."

"Come on." Max took her hand and twined his fingers with hers. "Unless you're going home for the holidays."

She'd been their tenant since June. In all that time, she never mentioned family, nor invited any friends over, including boyfriends.

"No home to go to." Her eyes darted to the large bag resting on the floor.

There was way more to her story than she was letting on, and being on her own bothered her more than her shrug suggested. He let it drop for the moment, glad for an excuse to spend more time with her. "That settles it." He wrapped his arm around her shoulder. "You're coming with us."

Sean reached across the table, taking her free hand. "I've been telling Mom about you since you moved in, Claire. If she finds out I didn't bring you with me, she probably won't let me in the door."

God, his boy was going to make some woman extremely happy someday. If it proved Claire was that woman, Max vowed he'd know when it was time to make his exit. "Now we have that settled," he said. "What are the three of us going to do the rest of the night?"

Chapter Two

Claire's stomach fluttered with Max's suggestion. She should really work harder to keep from imagining what it would be like to make love with her two roommates. With his arm settled on her shoulder and Sean holding her hand, it was hard to do.

She crossed her legs to ease the ache between them. At least if she was imagining what her guys looked like naked, she wasn't wondering what her family back in Maryville, Alabama would be doing this year for the holidays. *God*, she missed them, and the package they'd sent only added to the longing.

Claire leaned into Max, feeling his hard chest against her. Everything about him was a little rough. Gritty even. Which was why he was so good at his job. The people on his beat could relate to a cop who'd lived the hand-to-mouth existence they were trying to eke out. He was also good at getting underneath her skin. Her fingers traced his hard abs even as she admired his best friend to her right.

Sean wasn't any slacker in the workout department. Leaner than Max, he had the body of a swimmer with broad shoulders and tight hips. On more than one occasion, she'd been nearly late to class so she could get a glimpse of his bare chest as he came in from his morning run.

"I want to veg out in front of the television," she

said. *Sandwiched between you two.* They hung out eating pizza and watching movies at least once a week since she moved in with them. It was one of the things she'd miss most when she moved on.

"Only if Sean or I get to pick." Max used the hand that had been resting on her shoulder to mess up her hair. "Isn't that right?" He punched his buddy in the shoulder. "I declare tonight a no chick-flick movie night."

"Whatever Claire wants." Sean scrubbed a palm over his face. "After last shift, EMT school today, and then having to dress up like an idiot for the calendar, I'm beat." Frown lines furrowed his normally happy face. Even as he'd been coaxing her into spending Christmas with his family, she sensed his mind had been on something else.

Her two friends couldn't be more different. Where Sean was sweet, patient, and easy to talk to, Max had this whole strong, silent thing going for him when he wasn't ripping into someone with his wit. Her gaze darted between the two as they traded good-natured barbs. She couldn't stay in the dark place the package and letter from her hometown had put her in. Not when he was determined to make her laugh, and Max was heating her body to the boiling point.

Claire drained her cola in an attempt to cool down. The way Max played with her hair, his fingers dipping beneath her curls to massage her neck, sent tendrils of electricity straight to her core. They were everything she longed for in a guy, all rolled into two delicious packages. She wanted them. It was as plain as that. With the necessity to leave town looming, she was out of more subtle options for letting them know how she felt.

"Hey, let me get you a refill," Sean said. His hand trailed along her arm before he grabbed her empty glass and stood. As he did, her gaze darted to his crotch. She couldn't help it. It was right at eye level. And she was almost certain he'd been sporting a hard-on.

Max leaned in once he was out of earshot. "My boy there has a thing for you."

She couldn't get her hopes up the stars were aligned so that his attraction matched her own. "No he doesn't," she said, shaking her head. He was super sweet to her, but then again he was that way to everyone.

"And if I'm not badly mistaken, I think you've got the hots for Seany-boy as well."

Claire jerked up her chin. How could he tell? Other than some occasional ogling, she kept her attraction buried deep.

"Your pupils dilated when he touched you just now," he said, answering her unspoken question.

"Well, that might be true." So was the fact she was reacting to his touch as well. Her nipples were tight against the lace of her bra, adding to the overall achiness of her body. "But I'm not looking for anything long-term." The only sexual relationship she could manage right now was the one she had with her vibrator.

"Me either, sweetness."

Any question she had about whether he was coming on to her went up in smoke with his heated gaze. Claire placed her hand on his incredibly well-toned thigh, letting him know she wanted him right back. Her hand itched to creep toward the front of his pants, where she'd find Sean wasn't the only one with a hard-on. Everything she knew about Max screamed he'd be an amazing lover.

Her attention shifted as Sean returned with their refills. His guy-next-door smile made her want to see if she could put a different kind of grin on his generous lips. As for the type of lover he'd be, she'd bet her next paycheck he had rock-your-world potential, too. But would he want to play? At least she knew he wasn't completely averse to the idea of a threesome. With him still wearing the Santa's hat, a particularly naughty idea took root in her imagination.

****

Sean ran his fingers around the rim of his beer mug. He had to have something to do with his hands other than brushing Claire's dark hair from her face so he could see her warm brown eyes better. Her long tresses hung in sensual curls around her shoulders, but they hid her beautiful cheekbones and long lashes. She also disguised her curvy body behind bulky clothes. Ever since she walked into the bar, his imagination had been running through all kinds of scenarios where he got to see all of her ivory skin. *Hell,* he'd been dying to get his hands on her since she first walked into the house he and Max owned.

The way she fidgeted in her seat made him think something was off. As the three of them talked, her expression changed, like she'd made up her mind about something. He still wasn't prepared when she scooted off her seat and into his lap.

Claire twined an arm around his shoulders and leaned in. "I was wondering if I could tell Santa my Christmas list."

Jeez, he'd forgotten all about the red and white hat he put on for the photo shoot. She purred a particularly explicit wish in his ear that got his mind off the embarrassment. And turned his dick rock hard. Then she proceeded to detail exactly what she wanted. It involved both him and Max.

Sean shot a look at his buddy who arched his eyebrows in silent question. Max's taste in hook-ups ran along the lines of quick and kinky with a little sharing on the side. Had he put her up to this?

Claire was a lot of things—smart, sassy, and so sensual—one thing she wasn't, was a push over. She'd gone toe-to-toe with him over leaving a mess in their bathroom that proved that.

He'd wanted to hook up with her for months. The only thing that stopped him was her seeming lack of interest. *Boy*, was she good at playing things close to the vest. He'd also been hampered by the fact he wasn't good with no-strings-attached, not like Max who elevated hit-and-run to an art form.

What fueled her fevered need? He shoved that thought to the corner in favor of fulfilling Claire's wish. "Let's go." He grabbed her coat and led her outside into the cold. He turned back for a second to make sure his friend was following. "You parked out back?"

When they reached Max's truck, he helped settle her into the bench seat. It would be a tight fit, and Claire would have to straddle the gear shift. Thankfully, their house was only a mile from the bar.

"You okay in the middle?" he asked after climbing in after her. He hoped she'd get that he was asking about more than her comfort inside the truck's tight cab.

She ducked her chin. "I like being between you guys." Her gaze shifted between the two. "It makes me feel…"

"Wanted, safe," Sean finished for her. He had a gut feeling she never had a threesome before. He wanted to make her feel comfortable taking this risk with them. He also wanted to tell her he wanted more than this one time only event. He kept that tidbit to himself. "We're going to take good care of you."

After putting the truck in gear, Max moved his hand to her thigh. "Tell me. What did you say to our boy that got him sprinting out of the bar like someone set fire to an orphanage?" He pulled her in for a deep kiss. "Was it this?"

Her breath came in pants. "Yes." She reached back to take his hand and place it on her hip. "I want both of you to do that and more."

Sean reveled in the commanding way Max took over. Even more, he loved watching his best friend getting Claire excited. She threw herself into what they were doing. Was he seeing another side of her she'd kept hidden all these months, or was it something else? He should have felt guilty at the pleasure of watching them make out, but tapping into his voyeuristic side only added another level of heat to their tryst.

Max rubbed between her legs, making her squirm in the seat. The feel of her body rubbing against his, had Sean ready to bark at Max to drive faster. He couldn't wait to get her home so they could strip her out of her clothes and take turns making love to her.

"My turn." Sean tugged Claire his way.

He slid his hand up her leg, and then cupped her mound as he kissed her. Wanting to taste her, he licked at the seam of her mouth until she opened for him. She tasted minty, and as he stroked his tongue along hers, she practically purred. He fisted her hair, tilting her head back and absorbed her moans.

"Jesus, I'm going to wreck if you two keep this up." Max groaned as he pulled onto their street.

Despite his protest, Sean took his friend's hand, placing at the apex of Claire's thighs. "Do you like having the two of us getting her hot?"

Her hand slid up to his crotch. Sean thought it impossible he could get any harder. As she rubbed his dick, he swelled painfully against his zipper. "No, babe, you first."

"Please." Her brown eyes darkening with lust.

It made him certain there was more going on with her than a sudden need to get laid, like she was trying to lose herself in pleasure. He was more than happy to help her with that. He brought her hand back to his erection. "Anything you want; it's yours."

She traced the outline of his shaft, rubbing him from the outside. After a few strokes, he was teetering on the edge. Perspiration dotted his forehead. "Wait," he said, afraid he'd come in his pants. He covered her hand with his own.

"No," Max said, turning his attention from the road ahead. "I want to see him lose it."

Claire eagerly obeyed, going for Sean's zipper.

He levered his hips, letting her slide his jeans down. His heart pounded in his chest. Then she used the bead of pre-cum at the tip of his erect cock to lubricate the friction as she pumped his shaft with her fist. He gritted his teeth, determined to last longer than a few seconds. He even tried calling up baseball stats to delay the orgasm poised in his shaft. When she began fondling his balls in concert with long strokes, he was a goner. "Jesus, I'm coming." He groaned as cum shot from his dick. Through the blood rushing in his ears, he heard Max curse and then grind the gears of his truck.

Her eyes widened. "That was amazing."

His cheeks heated. "Oh yeah, you haven't seen anything yet." He reached for the hem of her blouse, pushing it up to reveal her lacy bra. He palmed her breasts. "So beautiful," he murmured. Weeks ago, he caught a glimpse of her wrapped in a towel as she came out of the bathroom. He pushed the twin globes together. Fucking between them played a prominent role in his fantasies as he got himself off. He leaned over placing a kiss to the top of each swell. Then he pushed down the black lace and trailed his tongue along the soft flesh before sucking the tip into his mouth.

Her groan of encouragement was all he needed and he spent the rest of the drive home alternating between gentle nips and strong pulls on her tits. It wasn't until Max brought the truck to a stop that he stopped worshipping Claire's breasts.

"We're home," his friend said, sounding more than a little relieved it was a short trip. "Make our girl come, Sean."

She *was* theirs—at least for the moment. He wanted to bring her pleasure, but he wanted Max to be a part of making her scream. He shot him a look, seeing dark lust on his friend's face. "Tell me what to do."

****

The Dominant in Max roared to life at his buddy's request. "Let's get her inside." As much as he was dying to see her pussy laid out for them like a delicious feast, he wouldn't risk having a neighbor pass by. He might get off on watching, but her body was for him and Sean alone.

As the thought flashed through his brain, he cursed inwardly. Once his instincts kicked in, his possessive tendencies weren't far behind, which is why he made it a point not to get emotionally attached to the women and men he bedded. She wasn't his any more than Sean was. He was in this to ensure those two got together. That was all. At least that was the lie he told himself.

The trio made it inside their house in a flurry of coats, gloves, and boots they kicked off on their way to the living room. Being impatient as well as possessive, Max scooped Claire into his arms and crossed the wooden floor to lay her out on their leather sofa. Settling at one end, he eased her head onto his lap and tugged her legs up on the cushions. "I want you to eat out her pussy," he told Sean.

Though not a true submissive, his boy took to directions like a champ. He began working her black trousers down her legs before Max barely had the instructions out.

She tilted her chin, looking up at him with warm eyes. Her lips were parted as her breath came in pants. Max swooped in for a quick kiss. "Relax, sweetness, we're going to make sure you get on Santa's naughty list." Naughty list indeed. Beneath her jeans, a small triangle of lace covered her mound. "Beautiful, but those need to get gone," he said brushing his fingers over the black fabric.

Sean snapped the strings at each hip, revealing a jagged scar that ran from one hip to the other. Max's gaze darted to his friend's, whose lust-filled eyes darkened with concern. It seemed their girl had seen more of the world's underbelly than she let on.

Claire opened her legs in a silent plea, effectively distracting the men from asking what had happened to her. In a flash, Sean's head was between her legs, making her gasp.

"Do you like him eating out your cunt?" he asked, pushing his cop instincts to the edge of his mind. For now.

"Yes." She sucked in a breath then arched her back. "It feels so good."

"Is our girl getting wet?"

Sean lifted his head, his mouth and chin glistening with her juices. "God, yes, so wet." He grinned. "Here taste her cream." He pumped two fingers into her channel then offered the pair up to Max who drew them into his mouth.

He savored her tangy-sweetness, and the feel of Scan in his mouth. As much as he wished it were his friend's cock and not just his fingers, Max didn't let that stop him from reveling in the pleasure of sucking Claire's juices off his friend's hand. "You taste like the ripest strawberries," he told her when he'd licked Sean's fingers clean. "Are you ready for us to fuck you senseless? Tell us now, otherwise I have a feeling once our boy here gets started it's going to be hard to rein him back in."

She arched her back. "More, please. I want it all."

Max met her gaze. Things were about to get serious between the three of them, and despite her naughty request, he wanted to make sure Claire was on board with what was about to go down. "Do you trust us?"

"Yes." Her voice came out low and husky.

He wanted to tell her to call him Sir, but they weren't there yet. Instead, he dipped his head for a quick kiss. "Good girl." Then he turned to Sean. "You heard her." Max hooked his palms under her knees.

Sean shot him a crocked smile. "Yes, sir." Then he dipped his mouth to her core.

Within seconds, her gentle moans became pants, and then groans as she screamed out her orgasm. Claire kicked back her head, her lips forming a sensual circle as Sean brought her orgasm to a peak. God, she was so responsive. He'd never have guessed beneath those bulky clothes and girl-next-door personality lay such a sensual creature.

When Sean continued to lap at her pussy even after her climax, she pushed against his head. "No more. It's too much."

Max was all over that. "No," he growled as he captured her hands and pulled them over her head. "You gave your pleasure over to us, so you'll take what we give you." He didn't know what prompted her to initiate this tryst, but he intended to make sure she didn't regret the decision.

Sean continued to suck on her clit and pump his fingers inside her until she screamed out another orgasm. When her cries softened to whimpers, Max shot another direction to his buddy: "Strip. I want to watch you fuck her."

Claire proved she was also a good direction follower as she scrambled to undo Sean's jeans. He guessed her first experience with Sean's hard dick had only whetted her appetite for more. Sitting upright against the back of the sofa, his cock jutted proudly from his hips. Proving he was a good Boy Scout as well as a good firefighter, he was already in the process of rolling on a condom.

Max's own cock throbbed with need as he watched her throw her leg across Sean's hips. His pulse raced as his palms made contact with her bare back. *God,* her skin was as soft as he imagined. Putting gentle pressure on her shoulders, he helped her take in his friend's length. Then he reached around from behind to palm her breasts. He rolled the tight buds between his thumb and fingers, adding the right amount of pinch.

Claire's head lolled back with pleasure. Leaning forward, he captured her mouth. Jutting his tongue into hers, he mimicked Sean as he fucked her pussy. They found a rhythm that worked for them. It began slow and easy and increased speed as both raced toward orgasm.

"I'm so close." Sean groaned. "I can't hold out much longer. Help me bring her."

Max chuckled, knowing how his buddy felt. Seeing those two in the throes of passion, he needed every ounce of his self-control not to press her onto Sean's chest, taking her rosette and making this a true three-way.

Instead, he reached around to rub the top of her bare cleft. As he teased her clit, his hand brushed against the crisp hairs at Sean's root. His fingers ached for more contact, wanting to give pleasure to his buddy as well. In Max's head he could see himself stroking Sean's long length as Claire sucked the head, or fondling his balls while her tight sheath wrenched an orgasm from him.

He redoubled his efforts to pleasure Claire. This was about her, not his selfish desires. Besides, his best friend might be sexually curious and a willing learner, but he'd never shown any signs of being bi.

The reality didn't stop Max from looking—or wanting. His gaze traveled from the beads of sweat dotting Sean's body, down his flexed forearms that bracketed Claire's body, and then they lowered to his friend's muscular thighs. Her arousal glistened as it seeped from her core and wetted Sean's tight sac. Max licked his lips. He lowered himself to the space between the sofa and the coffee table. One taste.

A guttural moan from Claire stopped him. She shook her head. "Oh, God, it's too much."

His index finger delved between her tight cheeks to massage her rosette. Her orgasm radiated throughout her body, making him wish he'd been the one to give it to her.

His own release poised at the ready. One touch from either of them would set him off. Only the sight of Sean's hard cock could draw Max's attention from the throbbing that pressed against his fly.

"Holy, fuck," Sean groaned. He held Claire tight against his hips as he bucked against her.

Max let out a breath and raked his hand through his hair. By some miracle, he'd been allowed to watch his friends making love. *And* managed to keep himself under control. He kissed the top of Claire's shoulders and caught her as she collapsed sideways on the sofa. "You were beautiful, sweetness," he crooned.

"She sure was," Sean echoed, leaning down for a kiss.

She bit her bottom lip and smiled. "But I'm not done yet. I want to make love with you, too, Max."

He clamped his eyelids closed—not making love—

fucking. He reminded himself of the situation so he wouldn't make the same mistakes as he had with David and Lydia, the couple he'd gotten involved with a few years back.

With that determination made, he opened his eyes. "You can have whatever you want." Except his heart. That he'd never risk again. Not for Claire, as sweet as she was. Not even for Sean, the buddy he cared more about than anyone else in the world.

Chapter Three

Claire should have felt sated from her recent orgasms. Instead, the aftershocks made her greedy. Her gaze darted to him. "Please, Max."

"Where do you want me to fuck you?" he asked, his suggestion open for interpretation.

Though she was hardly virginal, she'd never had anal sex. She used her vibrator back there a few times, and loved the sensation of fullness it gave. She stroked him from the outside of his jeans. Max could stand for maximum when it came to the cock department. "In the shower," she said, thinking she wasn't ready for his large size in her back hole.

He scooped her into his arms again and headed for the stairs. "You coming, Seany-boy?" he asked over his shoulder. He carried her up the stairs to the hallway bath the three of them shared. Then, after passing her off to Sean's waiting arms, he darted out of the room. He returned in seconds with a handful of condoms and began adjusting the water in the shower.

Built after World War II, their house had a single bath. At some point during the last few years, a previous homeowner remodeled the room, upgrading the shower to a space big enough for the three of them. After stripping out of his jeans, Max stepped into the spray. "Bring her here," he told Sean who was holding onto Claire like she was too precious to put down.

She slid down his hard body as he backed them under the spray. Between the recent orgasms and the adrenaline that came from being sandwiched between the two men, her legs felt too weak to hold her up. Both men reached for her as she stumbled.

"Hold onto our girl while I fuck her from behind," Max said.

"Holding on," Sean said, gripping her hips. "And never letting her go."

Claire's heart thudded, as she wished his words could come true. At least Max was on the same page with her, seeing their tryst as the expression of lust it was and not a romantic fantasy. His calloused palms abraded her skin as they slid from her shoulders to her ass. He kneaded the twin globes before slipping a single finger between her cheeks. "God, you've got an ass on you." He penetrated her core, pumping inside her a couple times. Then letting his finger slid along the perineum, Max teased the tight rosebud once again, sending licks of electric desire up her spine.

She let out a groan as his fingertip breached the tight ring of muscles.

"Looks like our girl likes a little back door play," Max said, chuckling darkly.

"Oh, she does, does she?" Sean said, tweaking her nipples. "What else does she like?"

Her head lolled back on Max's shoulder as she groaned loudly. The little licks of pain made her pussy clench.

"I think she likes a little pain with her pleasure," Sean said, answering his own question and flashing a dirty grin she'd never seen on his face before.

"I do," she admitted. Her cheeks heated, though it

seemed a little late in the game to wax shy. "The burn feels so good."

"You are playing with fire, little one." Max's breath tickled her ear even as his warning sent her pulse racing. "Sean, you show Claire some love, and I'll make sure to give her those little licks of pain she's so fond of.

"Fuck, yeah," he growled. He clenched his jaw and his cock stiffened with Max's command.

Clearly, she wasn't the only one who responded to their roommate's bossiness. It seemed as if the three of them were breaking all kinds of house rules, as they revealed things about themselves. Instead of igniting jealousy as the women in the bar had, the possibility her men might have a thing for each other eased some of her anxiety.

Tears pricked the back of her eyes. She shut them so Sean couldn't see the sadness and misinterpret her feelings. Maybe something good could come from their tryst, other than just a sweet memory when she left.

Max cocked her hips. "Widen your stance and wrap your arms around Sean," he said. Then his cock slid along her ass cheeks before slamming into her pussy.

"Oh, God." She drew in a breath, adjusting to his girth. Where Sean had been long with a flare to his head that rubbed along the ridges of her channel, Max's thick cock stretched her as he plowed into her. He pumped fast and hard, his thrusts driving her forward into Sean's body.

"You're so beautiful," Sean murmured. His cock rubbed against her clit while his fingers switched between tweaking her nipples and massaging her breasts that had grown heavy with need. "So soft and sweet, you're everything I imagined you'd be." He pressed gentle kisses to one shoulder while Max nipped the other.

"And so unbelievably wet," Max added, his cock stroking her g-spot with every thrust. "It's like nothing I've ever experienced."

Claire couldn't agree more. With their bodies caging her, she felt safe and whole for the first time in years. Then Sean's hand left her breast and trailed up her arm to run his fingers through Max's short hair. God, what a turn on that was. Her orgasm washed over her as she felt Max's thrusts become more urgent.

She clung to Sean's shoulders as Max climaxed. With her eyes clamped shut, she dug her fingers into his flesh as much to cement this moment in her memory as the need to brace herself against Max's relentless pounding against her ass. She let go of everything except the feel of his dick jerking inside her as Sean whispered sweet encouragements in her ear.

Max collapsed against her back. His warm breath tickled her neck as he recovered from his orgasm. Then he pressed a kiss to the sensitive spot behind her ear. "Goddamn, that was unbelievable."

The warm water cascaded over them, mixing with the scent of hot sex and her peppermint body wash, turning their glass-enclosed shower into an erotic paradise. If these were her last moments, she could die a happy woman. The thought chilled her to the core, causing her to shiver.

"Are you cold, sweetness," Max said, rubbing his calloused fingers over her arms.

Her body trembling, she stepped out of Sean's

embrace. "I'm fine." Claire got out of the shower and wrapped herself in the towel, but it did nothing to stop the icy shards of fear lancing through her. As she came down from her sex-induced high, reality swallowed all the pleasure she felt at making love with her two roomies. She'd used them to help her forget—which was a great plan as she'd thought of little else since she crawled into Sean's lap. On the other side of her mind-blowing experience, things looked a lot different. Especially as she caught the starry look in Sean's eyes.

God, Max was right. Sean was a happily-ever-after kind of guy, and she was a happy-for-the-next-hour kind of girl. Even now, Billy Townsend could be closing in on her. He vowed when he got out, he'd come looking for her. With his laser-like determination and his family's money, a little thing like moving and changing her appearance would only hold him off for so long. She bolted. What she'd done was wrong on too many levels to count.

"Wait," Max called as she fled the bathroom. Claire darted into her bedroom, but he was quick on her heels and blocked her from shutting the door. "Come here and let me hold you, little one." He caught her up in his arms. "Talk to me. Did we push you too far?"

His concern pricked her conscience. Max's go-to response was to fix everyone's problems, and Sean wasn't any better in the natural-born hero department. If either found out what happened to her—what might yet happen—they'd stop at nothing to protect her. "This is wrong." She pushed against his chest. Billy had already proven he didn't mind hurting others if they got in his way.

Max tilted her chin to look her in the eye. "There's

nothing wrong with what we did."

"What he said," Sean added, sandwiching her in the middle.

"Yes, it was. It was so very wrong." The feel of their wet, naked bodies against hers clouded her mind. Claire fought to get out of their embrace. The cold air hit her hard, sending her dashing for her bed. She crawled under the covers, pulling them over her head. On either side of her, the bed compressed with the weight of two large men.

Sean pulled the covers from her face. Concern darkened his eyes to the color of jade. "Because Max got me going?"

She wouldn't leave them thinking her reaction had anything to do with what happened between the two men. She levered up, taking their hands in hers. "No, I'm okay with that. I shouldn't have asked you to have sex with me."

He cupped her cheek. "You didn't ask me to do anything I didn't already want to do." His gaze shot to the other side of the bed. "Max, too."

"Listen to him, sweetness," he said, adding his hands to Sean's in pulling the covers from her. He traced a finger along her collarbone while Sean thumbed a still-tight nipple. "We'd do it again in a heartbeat if you'd let us."

Desire licked along her core. "It was wrong, and it can't happen again." Even if she wanted it more than she wanted her heart to keep beating. This wasn't about what she wanted. Or even needed. Claire beat back mercilessly against the urge to surrender to their caresses. She slapped away their hands. "Go away, dammit." She was only seconds from giving in.

Hurt flashed in Max's eyes before he hid it behind a mask of indifference. "Whatever you say, sweetness." He shoved off the bed.

Sean's face jerked to Max. "But…"

He snagged Sean by the wrist and tugged him away. "Let's get some clothes on your bare ass and leave our girl alone."

"I can make her understand."

"You heard the lady." Max shoved his friend from behind until he had them both out in the hall. "She's done with us." He closed her off from them, but even through the wooden door, she could still hear Sean's confusion.

"What did we do wrong?"

Nothing, she wanted to scream, but her resolve was too weak to test while two naked men stood outside her door. Tomorrow perhaps, when she'd put a little distance between her emotions and the best sexual experience of her life.

****

Max dropped the grip he had on Sean's shoulders. Touching his best friend's bare body wasn't helping him get his head screwed on straight. He stabbed a finger in his direction. "Don't go back in there," he told his friend who was still staring at Claire's closed door. The directive went doubly for himself. He'd never been one to cuddle after sex, but visions of the three of them spending the night together had filled his head ever since they'd been back at Guns 'N' Hoses. Wasn't irony just karma's equally bitchy twin sister? Instead of settling in for the night with the two people he cared most for, he was standing on the other side of the door buck-naked.

Sean didn't make a go for her door, but he wasn't heading off to his room either. "Something must have happened to make her want what we just did."

His words echoed Max's own thoughts. The one-eighty she'd done didn't mesh with the girl he'd known for the past few months. Then there were her scars to consider. "Maybe, but we have to let it go for now. You can try to talk to her again in the morning."

He'd known Sean had a thing for Claire, and likely having a taste of her was just enough to make him only want more. He checked in with his buddy's expression. Sure as shit. Resolve shown in those green eyes of his.

"I want her, Max."

He made up his mind to do now what he should have from the first. "I know, and if you want to go after her, I'll step back. Maybe she would be responsive to that." He reined in the urge, the one that screamed for both of his roommates. Those two had the best chance of making a go of it, and he'd be damned if he'd end up the third wheel again.

Sean shook his head, all his determination evaporating. "I don't know."

Max stepped inside the bathroom, snagging clothes off the floor. If he was going to have anything resembling a rational conversation, he couldn't do it if Sean's dick was on display. After passing his friend a pair of sweatpants, Max covered his desire with a little provocation. "What, not up for the challenge? You're too used to the women throwing themselves at you. You're going to have to work to get Claire. Give her the night to process what just happened."

He steered them down the hall toward their respective rooms. "In the morning, you can swoop in with your good-guy routine. I guarantee you, she'll be changing her social media status before the day is over."

Sean glanced back up the hall. "I'm not so sure. I get the feeling it will only allow her more time to rebuild that wall she has been hiding behind."

Max agreed. From day one, she'd been the perfect tenant—polite, considerate, and fun to hang out with. He sensed something dark hidden beneath her sweet charm. The image of the puckered scar flashed in his head. "If she does, you'll just have to scale the walls like the hero you are," he said before closing himself inside his room.

Chapter Four

The sound of movement outside her door stirred Claire from an uneasy sleep. After pushing the guys out of her room, she spent hours replaying every moment from her first kiss with Max under the mistletoe, to the door closing behind him and Sean.

Right before she heard the snow plow rumble down the street, she made a decision. First, she was apologizing to them. After that, she'd reach out to Mr. Blackwell, the attorney who five years earlier had created a new identity for her. She hadn't gone through with the change then, wanting to hold on to some vestige of her old life. Now it was her best option for staying ahead of Billy.

She got out of bed, wanting to catch at least one of the men before he left for work. As she planted her feet on the cold wooden floor, her head pounded as if she'd been on a bender. She had been in a way. Only instead of alcohol, she'd indulged in sexual excess followed by a tearful chaser. If her mother was there—after first being appalled at her oldest daughter's behavior—Sarah Mathews would say the pain between her daughter's ears was the down payment for her sins.

Sean opened the door, catching Claire in the same state of undress as he'd left her in the night before. His gaze raked over her before she snagged the comforter off the bed. "Good morning," he said smiling. "I made you coffee. Just how you like it, lots of cream and no sugar."

She tightened her grip on the covers to keep from accepting the mug. Or walking into his embrace. "You shouldn't have done that."

"I don't mind," he said, shrugging. He placed the mug on her nightstand. "I wanted to bring you something to wake you up. I know how hard it is for you to get up in the mornings."

Her stomach tied itself in knots, realizing what she had to do. Sean would no doubt mistake an apology as an excuse to persuade her last night hadn't been wrong. "No," she said, keeping all the affection she still harbored for him from her voice. "I mean you *shouldn't* have done that. I'm sorry for making you think I wanted more."

He shot her one of his lazy smiles. "I was hoping you'd changed your mind."

"I haven't." Immediately, she wanted to snatch back her words as his handsome features hardened. She took his hand to take the sting out of her rejection. "You're going to make some girl a great boyfriend someday."

So would Max. Separate they were incredible and together they'd rocked her to her foundation. Hours later, she could still feel the echoes of their caresses, which meant she needed to put some serious space between her and Sean.

He captured both her hands when she tried to pull away. His gaze caught hers as he pressed his lips to the back of her hand. He had the most expressive eyes she'd ever seen, and they telegraphed his desire before he uttered his next sentence. "I want you for more than just a quick fuck."

"I know." Problem was so did she, but her time with him was limited to however long it took Mr. Blackwell to send her new identity papers. Then she'd be off to wherever her bank account could take her. "I wish I could offer you the promise of something more, but I can't be with you."

Sean's jaw ticked. "What about Max? Do you want him instead?"

She shook her head. "Not instead, no."

"As well as?" he asked, arching his brows.

Claire couldn't leave him thinking she didn't cherish what happened between them. Likely, she'd spend the rest of her days replaying their time together both in and out of bed. "I loved what the three of us did together."

"Good," he said, nodding as if that settled things. "Because I don't feel right pushing him over to the side."

A vision of the way the two guys had been together flooded her mind. She'd sensed their relationship went deeper than mere friendship. But was there more between them? "Do you have feelings for Max?"

Sean studied the floor and several seconds ticked by. "I think I do," he finally answered. "Does that bother you?"

"God, no." It turned her on watching the sparks zinging between them. It would also make leaving easier if she knew they'd have each other. "You should talk to Max. See if he feels the same. He's a better bet than me."

****

Sean shook his head. First, he needed to get things

35

square with her, and then he'd deal with his newfound feelings for his best friend. "I'll talk to him, but I'm not ready to give up on you, Claire." He brushed her sleep-tousled hair away from her face. "Give me a chance to show you how good the three of us can be together."

A few tears shimmered in her brown eyes. "Please leave."

He sensed he'd pushed her as far as he could. "Okay." He backed away when he most wanted to kiss away her tears. "Call me tonight and let me know that you got home from work."

As he retreated into the hallway, he ran up against the other person who'd made sleeping last night an erotic marathon. "How'd it go?" Max asked.

Sean's gaze washed over his best friend's bare pecs then down to his lean torso. All that covered him was a towel wrapped low around his hips. Sean had seen Max in various stages of undress for years and never been aroused. It was as if what they'd done with Claire had stripped away a veil, forever changing how he saw his best friend. Confusion and desire tangled, sending his brain scattering in all directions. His body wasn't so confused by the myriad of emotions. A vision of Sean dropping to his knees in front of Max fired to life.

He clenched his eyelids, hoping it would help him keep his mind on the matter at hand. "Not great," he said. "She keeps saying she liked what we did, but that it can't happen again." His gut told him there was more to her resistance. "I think something bad happened to make her afraid, and it has to do with that scar."

"I don't disagree," Max said walking away.

"One more thing," Sean said, before Max shut his bedroom door. For a moment, Sean wondered if Max would ignore him.

Instead, he looked over his shoulder. "It doesn't mean you're gay."

Sean fought the smile curling his lips. The only way Max could have known what he was thinking was if the feeling was mutual. "I know that," he said. But it still didn't explain the dream he had of him bottoming for Max. Or what Sean would do about that fantasy.

****

No matter how much Claire threw herself into folding the table of brightly colored sweaters, or OCDing over racks of ladies' trousers and business suits, she couldn't keep her mind from replaying the conversation she had with Sean. Setting him straight was a too-little-too-late attempt to fix things. Even if he never understood her reasons, she'd done the right thing.

At noon, she had her first opportunity to call Mr. Blackwell. After that, she just hung out in the break room until it was time for her to return to the register. Regret and anxiety soured her stomach as she walked through the Women's Department.

"I can help whoever is next," she said, plastering on a smile. At least there were enough customers to keep her mind off her problems. When they hit a lull, Claire reached for a pile of clothes that needed to be returned to their correct departments.

"Wait, I almost forgot," Zoe, her coworker, said. "Some guy was here earlier asking for you."

Claire's pulse soared to triple digits. Her first thought was that Sean had come by wanting to resume their earlier conversation. She quickly dismissed that idea since he was scheduled to be at fire station for the next twenty-four hours. Could it have been Max? "What did he look like?"

Zoe shrugged. "I don't know. Average height, brown hair, late twenties."

That let Max out. Nothing about him was average. She didn't know any other man who'd be looking for her. *Except.* Pin pricks of icy anxiety danced over her scalp.

She drew in a steadying breath. It could be a customer she'd helped, or someone from class. She continued with her list of men who could want nothing more than help buying a Christmas present for the woman in their life. "What did you say to him?"

Zoe shrugged. "That you were on break and would be back in a few minutes."

Claire scanned the store for a guy with light brown hair, a charming smile, and the twisted mind of a sociopath. It had been nearly six years since she laid eyes on Billy. He could have changed his appearance in that length of time. She certainly had. The plastic surgeon had done a great job fixing her broken nose. She also dyed her naturally blonde hair a dark brown and wore colored contact lens to change her blue eyes to brown.

She drew in several more breaths. She was safe for now. It wasn't like Billy could haul her out of the store. Claire poured her energy into getting through the next several hours till she could leave the store. That did leave her the problem of the bus ride home and the six blocks between the bus stop and her house. "I'll stay to straighten up," she said when the last customer left at nine that evening.

After her final encounter with Billy, when he'd left

her for dead on the porch of her family's modest house, she spent a week in the hospital. After returning home, it took her weeks to leave the house and months before she could walk down a street without bolting every time the wind blew.

Once Billy was sent to Evergreen Psychiatric Hospital, she should have been able to start the healing process, but the Townsend family continued to harass her. Finally, sick of being scared to leave her house, she made the decision to leave. Not exactly how she expected to spend all the money she'd earned playing the piano in weddings, ballet practices, and the church her family attended, but she'd been more than thankful for the option it afforded her.

When she'd straightened up the entire department, she asked the store's security guard to walk her to the bus stop at the far end of the mall's parking lot. Every muscle in her body tightened as she settled in a seat near the front of the bus. This was no way to live.

The bus finally reached her stop, and her pulse thrummed in her ears as she walked up the aisle. Just six blocks, that's all she had to do. "Good night," she said, to the driver, stepping into the cold.

"Be safe," the middle-aged man responded.

"You bet." Drawing on the months of self-defense lessons she'd taken at the Student Union, Claire kept to the pools of light cast by the streetlamps. She walked with purpose, her head turning to scan the dark corners created by the close together houses. When she'd gone a block and a half from the bus stop, the dark figure of a man appeared in her peripheral vision. Wearing a lightweight jacket, the collar pulled up against the wind, it was impossible for her to gather anything more than it was a male—and that he was following her.

She gripped the Asp in her pocket and picked up her pace. Max would be pissed as hell at her for having the telescoping baton. At the moment, it seemed a fair trade off. Besides she had no intention of letting him find out she had the illegal weapon or a stalker. If she dragged Max into this mess, he'd only want to go all alpha male on her and start solving her problems.

Finally, Claire reached her goal. From the moment she'd first seen the post-war house it felt like home. Its red brick and bow-front windows called to her. Instead of stepping off the sidewalk and opening the little picket gate, she walked on past. If this was Billy following her, she couldn't risk giving away where she lived. She hiked her purse further on her shoulder and headed for the coffee shop at the end of the block.

"We're closed," the barista announced as she stepped inside.

"Oh, all right," she said, coming up with plan B while she watched for the guy from the window. Plan C was to call nine-one-one, which she would totally do if she got proof her experience tonight was anything more than her overactive imagination. She'd failed to listen to her fear once before, and it nearly cost her life.

Seconds later, she caught sight of the guy as he stepped into a pool of light. She got a good enough look at him that she'd remember if she saw him again but not enough to tell if it was Billy. Then the only positive thing that had happened to her all day occurred. A bus pulled up to the corner and her green-jacketed shadow boarded it.

Claire was out the door of the coffee shop and headed for home as the bus pulled away.

She shoved the key into the lock with a sense of triumph, reengaged the alarm, and shrugged out of her coat. Adrenaline took over her body. Hands trembling and stomach churning, she barely made it to the toilet before she threw up. The months she'd spent with Sean and Max lent her a measure of security that was a relief after years of looking over her shoulder. She stripped out of her clothes and after turning the shower on, crawled in under the hot spray.

The warm water should have eased her trembling muscles. Instead, all she could think about was what Sean and Max had done to her. They'd been spectacular taking turns fucking her, and the tentative caresses they gave each other turned her on better than she ever imagined. She never before caught any vibe between the two friends, but even in her lust-soaked haze, she couldn't miss the heated looks they exchanged.

Speaking of Sean, his ringtone sounded as she turned off the water. Grabbing a towel, she reached for her phone from the pile of clothes on the floor. "Hello."

"Hi, Claire," he began sounding as hesitant as she felt.

"Hi, yourself," she said, reveling in his voice. "How's your day going?"

"Long, busy. We got a call for a small fire, and a couple car accidents. Nothing serious, but good experience all the same, especially since I got to start an IV on one of the passengers before we transported him to the ER," he said, some of his usual cheerfulness returning.

"Awesome?" she said, not quite sharing his enthusiasm for emergency medicine.

"Well, it was for me, but maybe not so much for

Melissa Klein

the others." He cleared his throat. "I want to ask you a favor."

She gripped the phone, sending up a prayer it was a request she could grant. "What is it?"

"Would you help me bake Christmas cookies for the station party on Friday?"

"Of course," she said, hopeful this would give her a chance to repair the damage she'd done.

"Tell me what ingredients I need to buy to make sugar cookies."

"Give me a second," she held the phone between her ear and shoulder, "I just got out of the shower, and I'm about to lose my towel."

"Jesus, Claire, I didn't need that visual."

"Shit." Why did she say that? "I'm sorry."

"Stop," Sean barked. "I told you last night and again this morning, I've got no regrets and neither does Max. I just meant that I'm walking through the day room, and I don't want the crew getting a look at my hard-on through my sweats."

Now she was the one getting the visual. "What are you doing out of uniform?"

"I'm headed to my bunk," he said. "The rest of the guys are watching a movie, but I wanted to get some shuteye."

Guilt pricked her conscience. "I guess I'm not the only one short on sleep. I should probably let you go."

"There's something else I wanted to ask you," he said before she could hang up.

"Okay," she said, sensing a question she wasn't going to want to answer.

"Are you into Max?"

"It's not like that. I just can't start anything right

42

now."

"Oh," he said. "So you like me, too."

"Yes, Sean, I like you." If circumstances were different, she could see herself learning to love him.

"Jeez, no wonder I can't keep a girlfriend I sound like I'm in middle school."

"You do not. I'd be proud to be your girlfriend, if I was in that place in my life."

"Oh, really," he said, all his typical humor pouring back into his voice. "And as my girlfriend would you let me go down on you or fuck between those beautiful tits of yours?"

Her clit ached remembering the way he'd teased her to orgasm. "Now you're the one getting me all hot and bothered." She crawled under her covers, letting the towel fall to the floor.

"I'm in the bunkroom all by myself, and guess what I'm doing."

"Are you trying to have phone sex with me?"

"You bet. Just the sound of your voice gets me hard. I'm lying here all alone wishing this was your hand stroking my cock."

His cock had been like velvet over steel, and she'd loved tracing the vein that ran the length. "Me, too, Sean." She needed this escape after the terror of the last hour. "I wish I was with you right now, because if I was I'd take you into my mouth and suck you. I'd twirl my tongue around your ridge then suck you until you scalded my throat with your cum."

Claire rubbed her clit as she described how she wanted to give him head. Dipping a finger into her cunt, she coated her clit with her arousal. "After that, you know what I'd like for you to do?"

"What, Claire? Tell me."

"I'd want you to go down on Max. Would you do that?"

"God, I'd love that, but only if you watched."

"I'd let you and Max take turns fucking me from behind. You liked that didn't you? The three of us making each other feel good, would you like that?" She sure as hell did. In fact, it sent her over the edge. Rubbing her clit hard and fast, she rode the crest of her orgasm to Sean's accompanying groan. From the other end of the phone came the unmistakable sounds of him climaxing.

"I think I blew a blood vessel in my brain I came so hard," he said, breathless.

"Don't do that," she said feeling a lot more quivery than she usually did when she masturbated.

"No, that's a good thing. I like the way you make me feel, Claire. I like it a lot."

She snuggled under the covers as fatigue overtook her. "Me, too."

"Can I get in bed with you when I get off duty in the morning?"

Her heart ached. "I don't know."

"I know you have to work all day tomorrow, so I won't wake you. I just want to hold you."

While she'd made them both feel better for a few minutes, in the end she'd only given him false hope. "Sean, that's not a good idea."

"Okay, if that's how you want it, I'll go along with it for now. But I'm not giving up on you and neither is Max."

That's what she was afraid of.

Chapter Five

Two days after his hook up with Sean and Claire, Max pulled his truck into the driveway and killed the engine. It was a minute before he could force himself to get out. Not only was he bone tired, but he wasn't ready to face either of his roommates. "Idiot," he swore aloud. "Just rip off the bandage."

Unlocking the back door, he let himself into the mudroom just off from the kitchen. A chirp signaled the two had activated the house's alarm system. While Sean sometimes forgot, Claire never failed to lock both the deadbolt and reset the alarm, one more way the two of them were alike.

Laughter cut off Max's greeting. He froze in the doorway, taking in the scene. At least they weren't going at it on the kitchen table, but what they were doing was nearly as gut wrenching. They were baking, like some couple who'd been together since high school and were as close as two people could be.

"Stop that," Claire said, swatting Sean's hand as he snagged a handful of candy they were using to decorate cookies. "Do you want these to take to the station party or not?"

"I do. I just can't keep my hands out of the bag." He pulled her in for a deep kiss. "Or off you."

"Don't," she said, pointing a finger at him. "That was one of the stipulations for me helping you with this. No fooling around."

"I'm sorry," he said, not sounding sorry in that least that he'd not only kissed Claire but copped a feel as well.

This is what Max wanted. It was. Really. He just wished he could stop wanting to join them.

"I can't help myself," Sean continued. "I was thinking about that phone call last night. I'm never going to look at the bunk room the same way again."

"So you liked it," Claire said, smiling widely. "What part exactly did you like the best, when you told me how you wanted to fuck between my tits or when I described you giving Max a blow job."

Max's heart skipped a beat. It honest to God skipped a fucking beat. Then his dick got so hard he thought it might break through the fly of his pants. Not only did they have phone sex, they'd included him in their little fantasy.

"Definitely the blow job," Sean said. "I want him, too, Claire. I want the three of us to be together. It's all I've thought about since the other night."

"Did you talk to Max like I suggested?" she asked.

He couldn't take another second of the two of them plotting to get him to play along with their little game. Even if he'd been in love with his best friend for years and wanted to bury himself so deep in Claire's body she'd never want to let him go, he wouldn't be used by the two of them to help work out their little kinky scenes.

"You two certainly have made a mess," Max said, stepping into the kitchen. "I hope you were planning on cleaning up afterward."

Sean pulled away from her and began studying the

floor like the answers to the world's problem were hidden in the black and white tiles. "Of course."

Claire folded her arms across her chest. "What crawled up your butt and died."

"Nothing." Max scrubbed his eyes. "I'm just cold and tired."

"Come here," she said, opening her arms to him. "You shouldn't have to come home to your friends acting like kids."

He held up a hand to ward Claire off as she took as step toward him. "I'm fine. I just need a shower and some sleep." As badly as he wanted her, he'd crumble if she laid a hand on him.

"I brought home some Mexican from that place around the corner you like," Sean added. "Do you want me to nuke you a plate."

Max didn't bother to answer, didn't take the much-needed shower either. Instead, he climbed the stairs to his room and face planted on the bed. Pulling the covers over his head, he prayed sleep would catch up to him fast.

****

Sean winced as the kitchen door slammed. "You think he overheard us talking?"

Claire's eyes were wide as she nodded. "I'd say that was a pretty good guess."

He let his chin fall to his chest. "Shit. This was so not the way I planned for Max to find out." If things had gone according to plan, he'd get her comfortable with more than phone sex and then work on bringing Max back into the equation. Instead, it seemed all he could manage was a one-step-forward-two-steps-back scenario.

"That doesn't mean he doesn't want the same thing," she said, then shot him a sweet smile. "Go hash things out. I'll finish up down here."

Sean pecked her on the cheek. Maybe his friend's eavesdropping was only a minor step back, especially as it seemed Claire was eager to work things out between the three of them. "You're a peach," he said, bolting out of the room.

When he reached the upstairs, he walked in Max's room without knocking. "Hear me out."

"Fuck off. I've crashed."

Sean wasn't going to be put off that easily. He fumbled for the light switch, flooding Max's Spartan room with light. "It's only been a couple minutes. You can't have gotten to sleep that fast."

Max levered up. "Make it quick."

He froze by the side of the bed. Their friendship had always been an easy one. Had he ruined that? He clenched his fist and dove in. "I want to be with you. I want us to do things I never imagined doing with another guy."

Max scowled from beneath hooded eyes. "Shut the fuck up."

Sean blinked a couple times. He expected his friend to offer some explanation about things getting out of hand the other night, but not this anger. Had he read Max's signals wrong? He thought for sure the electricity zinging between them had gone both ways. *What a clusterfuck.* "Aren't you bisexual?"

Max shrugged. "I don't like labels, and it's not all men. It depends on the guy."

Sean felt like someone had punched him in the gut. "And I'm not one of them." Man, he'd made an ass out of himself as well as putting their friendship in jeopardy.

Max tugged him down to the edge of the bed. "It's not that."

Even as he told himself not to hold out hope, his imagination conjured up the image of Max kissing him. Or even better, Sean kissing Max. His cock stirred thinking about pressing his lips to Max's, then diving in and plundering his mouth. As he gripped the bedcovers to keep from initiating the contact, frustration boiled inside him. "I don't know what to do. I've never had feelings for another guy."

The leash he kept on the impulse slipped. He palmed the back of Max's head, bringing their mouths together. His lips were full, but that's where the softness ended. Rather than letting Sean take the lead, within seconds Max's tongue slipped inside his mouth. Their tongues dueled before he relented and let Max have the lead. When he finally broke the kiss, they were both breathing heavily. "Goddamn," Sean breathed. He trailed the hand that had been on Max's shoulder down his chest. Then he cupped his best friend's erection, stoking him from the outside of his sweats. Sean didn't know what felt better, being right or the feel of Max's length against his palm.

****

It took every ounce of Max's self-control not to flip Sean over and fuck him senseless—and not just because he had never yielded the lead to anyone. He'd hidden his feelings for Sean for the past four years, fucking everyone who'd let him in an effort to hide that the one person he wanted was now gripping Max's cock. "Stop," he finally managed after beating his lust into submission.

"What?" Sean's wide gaze met his. "You were into it. I could tell."

Into it didn't begin to cover how it felt, but ultimately he had to let his mind win out over his dick. "It shouldn't have happened. I'm sorry."

Sean raked his fingers through his blond hair. "If one more person tells me that, I'm totally going to lose my shit." He stabbed at finger at Max. "I kissed *you*, remember."

"You're curious. This thing with Claire's got you confused," he said, cutting the air with his hand. "That's all."

Sean jutted out his chin. "Don't tell me what to feel, man. I liked it."

"Of course you did. I'm good," Max said smiling.

"You're also a bit of an ass." Sean punched his shoulder. Then he ducked his chin. "But I wouldn't mind doing more."

Problem was a *little* more would never be enough. Besides, Max still wasn't convinced Sean had discovered another facet of his sexuality. "I'm not going to be your little experiment. And do me a favor, leave me out of any of your and Claire's little phone sexcapades. I don't like being your little kink."

"It's not like that," Sean said, reaching for Max's hand. "I want the three of us to be together again."

He clenched his eyes to block out the image of them in the shower. "You mean like another couple hook-ups and the two of you get to be a couple and I get left the odd man out." He'd been there, done that. *No fucking thank you.*

"Is this about that couple you were involved with?"

Max huffed. "This is exactly about them."

He met David and Lydia at the BDSM club where he was a member. He'd fallen hard for the couple, loving their openness. It took him six months to realize all he was to them was a guy to fulfill Lydia's love of double penetration and David's need to have his ass screwed a couple times a week. Neither wanted a third on a permanent basis, and when it came time for them to settle down, he was shoved to the side.

"We would never do that to you."

"Not on purpose you wouldn't, but what happens when you and Claire want to make things permanent? Where does that leave me?"

Sean shook his head. "I don't think she wants that." When he met Max's gaze, anxiety shadowed his gaze. "I keep expecting to wake up one morning to find she's disappeared on us."

Thankful for the change in direction the conversation was taking—even if it was only moving on to another difficult topic—Max nodded. "I know what you're talking about. Our girl's a bank vault of secrets." Despite the clusterfuck they'd made of their friendship, he worried about Claire. To someone like him, who had both firsthand experience in subterfuge as well as professional training at spotting deceit, it was obvious their girl was keeping some major darkness tucked away.

Sean gnawed on his bottom lip. "Will you help me find out what's going on then?"

He bumped his friend's shoulder. "Of course. Just leave me out of the romantic equation."

"You're not willing to give ménage another chance?"

"Haven't you heard the definition of crazy is doing the same thing and expecting different results?" Max said, knowing full well he needed to heed the adage.

Chapter Six

The night after the little kitchen scene, Claire burrowed deeper into the afghan as if the wool and darkness of the living room were a refuge. An hour ago, she'd seen the man again on her way home from the grocery store. Dressed in the same lightweight jacket as the other day, he trailed behind her—slowing or accelerating his pace to match hers. Like before, she made a detour to the coffee shop, returning home only when he boarded a bus at the corner stop.

The logical part of her brain insisted this man, who was the right age and height to be Billy, could also be any number of men who resisted dressing appropriately for the weather. She ignored that voice. It had steered her wrong before, telling her to trust a man with a disarming smile. Instead, she listened to the fear. It would keep her alive until her papers could be delivered in three days.

She jolted as her phone vibrated on the coffee table across from her. Her hand shaking, she switched off the ringer after looking at the screen—Sean again. With her threadbare resolve to handle her own problems, she didn't have the will not to ask for his help, or resist his sultry voice for another round of thought-diverting phone sex. She clenched her eyes at the damage she'd caused to not only her relationship with the men but their once-easy friendship as well. Instead of a sweet indulgence or giving her roomies a nudge toward each other, she made things worse.

Claire snapped on the television, hoping to lose herself in a holiday special—one that would make her laugh or give her reason to believe Christmas was the time for miracles. Flipping through the channels, her attention caught on a local news reporter's words.

"A young woman was found dead this afternoon in an alley behind a nightclub on Trade Street."

Claire paused with her finger on the remote. The address was one street over from the bar she and the guys frequented and part of Max's beat. Ordinarily, she avoided watching the news. Having been the subject of not only gossip but news reports that ran as far away from her Alabama home as Atlanta and New Orleans, she had her fill of drama hungry reporters.

"Police say the woman, who was in her early twenties, was raped before her assailant stabbed her in the abdomen over a dozen times," the solemn-faced reporter stated.

Instinctively her hand went to her belly, rubbing the jagged scar that ran from hipbone to hipbone. Claire forced herself to listen to the whole report, hoping for a detail that would rule this out as another senseless act of violence, not further proof that Billy had followed her to Chicago. No such luck. As the reporter informed the viewers this was the third in as many days, Claire's scalp prickled with anxiety.

Just as her finger paused over the power button, the camera panned to the background where several CPD unies were working. She scanned the screen, her gaze zeroing in on Max. Even dressed in a thick coat and his uniform cap pulled down to his brow, she couldn't miss the powerful way he moved. The need to reach out to him washed over her. All she had to do was ask, and he'd stop at nothing to keep her safe, even if it put his own life in jeopardy.

There'd been other men in her life like that. Her father cashed in part of his retirement so she could start over in a town where the Townsend Family didn't rule like medieval gentry. Her younger brother, Breandan had gone after Billy in the courtroom and had to be restrained by Sheriff's deputies. Even the shady attorney, Mr. Blackwell, bent the law in order to protect her. She wouldn't put Max in that position.

Hitting the mute button, Claire laid her head on the sofa's arm, drawing in slow breaths to keep panic at bay. Where the breathing techniques failed, planning how to keep her guys from being caught up in her ugly past succeeded. Before fatigue finally pulled her under, she made the decision to move to a hotel until her papers came.

****

Max finally made it home after a shift that made him wonder about his career choice. He prayed he'd never become completely immune to the effects of his job, even as he wished to erase the vision of the young woman's bloody body. Her similarity to Claire hit too close to the bone for that to happen.

He shrugged out of his parka, hanging it on the peg in the mudroom just the way Claire liked. She changed a lot of things in the months she'd been their roommate. Most were good, like the bench she bought for them to use while they pulled on and off their shoes. He'd also come to love how she sent him off to work after extracting a promise that he'd be careful. His mind flashed to Sean's expectant look the other morning—other changes not so much. It was dead wrong of her to fill his mind with false hope that there'd be a happily ever after. Max couldn't offer him a relationship any more than it seemed she could.

First thing tomorrow morning, he would have a little conversation with Claire about her stringing Sean along. It was one thing for her to take center stage in Max's dreams. That was on him. His buddy was still holding out hope for a real relationship.

Stepping into the living room, he found her curled up on the sofa—the television on. She looked like a goddess resting with her feet up and her light brown hair spilled loose around her shoulders. No wonder Sean was willing to beg for a few scraps of her attention.

Max stalked across the wooden floor. "Listen up."

She jolted like someone had hit her up with a couple hundred volts of electricity. Then cowering on the edge of the sofa, she shielded her face with her hands.

Her fear as she shrank back from him shamed him. "Goddammit." He raked his fingers through his hair. "I'm sorry, sweetness." Maybe he should wait until he was in a better mood before he talked to her. Between the scene he'd witnessed earlier and his mounting sexual frustration, it'd be sometime next spring before that happened. Max planted his ass on the coffee table. He'd say what he needed to, then get the hell out of there. "I want you to either set Sean straight once and for all or fuck him. I don't care which you do."

The fear in her eyes changed to anger. Claire crossed her arms over her chest and glared at him. "I can see how much you don't care."

Their little kitten was feeling as feisty as he was, but she could hiss all she wanted. He cared about her—more than he wanted to admit—but Sean was his best friend. "I won't stand by and watch you hurt him."

Her shoulders slumped. "I'm trying not to, Max. I've tried talking to him." She waved her arms in the air. "I've tried avoiding him. He's a little hardheaded if you haven't noticed."

She had a point. During their freshmen year in high school, he approached Max in the homeroom they shared. Sean had been a short, skinny kid back then with a geeky reputation that preceded him, but he stuck out his hand and introduced himself. Max hit him up with some snarky comment that typically worked at keeping people away. But not Seany-boy, he kept right on talking like they weren't the two most unlikely friends God ever imagined.

This was different. "Try harder."

Her lips compressed to form a thin line. "Are you done reaming me out?"

"No." He grabbed her hand and placed a canister of pepper spray in her palm. "I want you to keep this on you when you go out. There's someone out there attacking young women, and I don't want you to be his next victim."

She drew in a sharp breath as her eyes widened. She'd seen the news report, had probably been watching it earlier and that was the reason she'd been so frightened. Claire drew her knees to her chest.

"Shit." This was why he had no business attempting a relationship with anyone. He didn't have the first fucking clue how to be gentle. He brushed a hand over her hair. "It's okay."

She swatted him away. "Don't touch me."

Ignoring her, he wrapped an arm around her shoulders. "Breathe with me, sweetness." He mimed taking deep, slow breaths. "That's it."

Guilt ridden for causing her panic attack, he held her while she struggled to breathe. He slid a hand under her knees and was relieved when she let him pull her onto his lap. "I didn't mean to scare you."

Max's gut told him something other than the news report prompted her fear. His mind flashed to the scars along Claire's belly. They weren't the same as the woman who'd been found murdered on Trade Street. But when coupled with the way she struggled to breathe, they confirmed his suspicions. She'd suffered horrific violence in her past.

"You're safe. I'm not going to let anything happen to you." Whatever their issues at the moment, he'd stop at nothing to protect her. Over and over he murmured soothing words while he massaged circles over her back.

After a few minutes coaxing, her trembling stopped. "I'm fine now," she said, pulling out of his embrace. Claire thumbed away the tears from her cheeks. "I guess I've been watching too many police dramas," she said with a weak laugh.

He wanted to call her on the lie nearly as much as he wanted to kiss her until she divulged the secrets she was keeping. Max gripped the edge of the coffee table instead. "Sure thing." If she didn't trust him, he wasn't going to push where he wasn't wanted.

She held up the canister. "I promise to keep the pepper spray on me." Then she drew in a breath. "I'm also putting an end to things with Sean."

Max wanted to make sure they were perfectly clear. "So, no more phone sex?"

Her cheeks turned pink. He hadn't meant for her to know he'd been eavesdropping, but as long as she left Sean with an ounce of hope, he'd keep hanging on.

Desire shone in her eyes. For all that Claire looked like the goody-two-shoes, she was a temptress beneath the surface. Her eyes widened for an entirely different reason than they had moments ago.

"Does it turn you on, reliving what Sean and I did to you?" he asked.

She clenched her eyelids. "Yes." She breathed the words.

Max could no longer resist the call of her body. He tilted her chin. "Tell me what you two talked about." He brushed her long hair from her face. "Do you get yourself off while Sean talks dirty to you over the phone?"

"I do." She licked her lips. "He makes me so hot I can't help it."

Neither could he apparently. He leaned in to whisper. "Where does he put that big cock of his?"

"In your mouth." She purred.

Max froze, afraid if he moved a muscle he'd do something both of them would regret. Hearing they included him in their dirty conversation set off all kinds of sexual fireworks inside him. He wanted a repeat of the other night despite knowing what would happen if it did.

He brushed a thumb across her cheek. "Claire, if you don't want me to take you right here on the sofa, you better high-tail it up to your room."

She drew her sweatshirt over her head, revealing lovely ivory skin. Then meeting his gaze, she reached behind her back to unfasten her bra. Her nipples tightened in the cool air. She raised her chin offering him a smoldering look. "You want this as much as I do."

Max swallowed. No, after the shitty day he'd had, he *needed* to bury himself inside her. The urge to pull her down to the rug beneath him welled inside. In his mind, he'd already stripped her out of her clothes and was pounding inside her. "I don't do easy," he warned. "There's no other way with me."

Lust shimmered in her brown eyes as Claire bit her bottom lip. Slipping off the sofa, she turned her back to him. "Take me like this," she said, and then she shimmied out of her sweats. Her back narrowed to the waist, where her hips flared gently.

He ran his hands up the backs of her thighs before kneading the twin globes of her ass. He longed to tease her hidden rosebud. Instead, Max arched over her back. "Are you sure, sweetness?" He reached around her, tweaking her nipple between his fingers. "Be very sure this is what you want."

"Please." She begged, grinding her ass onto his erection.

Max set a record for the fastest undressing. Then after fumbling in his wallet for a condom, he sheathed himself. He nudged her legs apart. Then he slid his cock between her cheeks before pushing into her pussy. "God, you're so wet." He pulled out nearly to the end before slamming himself inside her.

Claire slid forward with his thrusts until she widened her stance. She arched her back into his thrusts.

He released the hold he'd had on her breast, his hand sliding down to tease the top of her sex. "That's it." She purred. He circled her clit with his finger in time to his punishing thrusts.

Fisting her hair, Max levered her face upward. He captured her mouth for a bruising kiss. The urge to mark her overtook him. He nipped his way across her cheek before clamping down on the tender spot where her neck and shoulder met. Her groans of pleasure spurred him on. He alternated between soothing the pain he caused with swipes of his tongue and metering out more biting nips along her delicate skin. When this was over, she'd have a line of love bites that would last for days.

She cried out as an orgasm overtook her. Max increased the tempo, driving her on to a second orgasm as his own release boiled up. Grasping her hips, he pounded out his orgasm. "Fuck," he shouted. His vision narrowed as he rode the crest. He collapsed on top of her, both drawing in heavy breaths as they recovered.

Fast on the heels of his release, reality washed over him. Guilt curled in his gut, burning its way up his throat. Regardless of what Claire claimed, Sean thought of her as his girl. And Max had just fucked her into oblivion. Right there on the floor like a dog.

Holding the condom in place, he pulled out of her. By the time he returned from disposing of it, she'd redressed. Standing by the stairs, she said, "I'm checking into a hotel until I can find a new place to live. I'll be gone before Sean gets back from the station."

He snagged her hand, stopping her from taking the

stairs. "Don't do that. It'll kill him." Like finding out his best friend had fucked his girl wouldn't. "Give him a chance. He's a good guy."

****

Claire massaged the ache in her chest. *So are you, Max.* Telling him that would only make her departure more difficult. "I can't." She turned her face, hoping to hide how much she wanted her answer to be different.

"Is it because you think Sean is gay?" he asked, snagging her hand. "Because he's not."

"That's not it at all. I'm just not in that place in my life right now." She had to find a way to make this right with Max. Otherwise, he'd carry around the burden of guilt when he wasn't to blame for the mess. Nothing she thought to say seemed right. She wouldn't lie and the truth would only make things worse. "It's complicated," she finally said.

He folded his arms across his bare chest. "Then explain it. I may not be as smart as Sean, but I'm not stupid."

"I never said you were." Claire blew out her breath and prayed she'd get at least this part right. "I have some things in my past I thought I'd buried. I found out recently that they're not as dead and gone as I'd hoped."

Max's eyes narrowed.

"It's nothing illegal in case you were worried you were harboring a fugitive or something."

The muscle in his jaw ticked. "Give me some credit, Claire. I may not know everything about you, but I know you're not a criminal."

"Thanks." She offered him a weak smile. "I couldn't stand it if my past blew back onto you two."

"And you won't tell me what it is." His eyes darkened.

"I can't."

"Right now," he said, his nostrils flaring. "It's taking every bit of my self-control not to put you across my knee and paddle the story out of you."

God, his threat shouldn't have made her pussy clench like that. Especially as he'd just driven her to two screaming orgasms. "Stop it. Your threats won't work on me."

"Don't tempt me, little one." Max brushed the back of his hand across her cheek. "Promise me you'll stay here through the holidays. I'll make Sean back off, and I'll be on my best behavior, too."

"I'll stay," she said, knowing it was a promise she couldn't keep.

Chapter Seven

Late the next morning, Sean finally pulled into his driveway. Putting the car in park, he stifled a jaw-cracking yawn. "No, Mom. I haven't forgotten about the party tonight," he said speaking to her on his Bluetooth. After working a house fire all night, he was surprised he remembered his own name.

"Tell Max I've ordered extra baby quiches from the caterer just for him," she said.

"I will," he answered, although there was no guarantee his best friend would even stand still long enough to listen to the relayed message. Ever since they kissed the other night, Max had managed to avoid being in the same room with him, much less actually getting pinned down for a conversation.

"Is Claire still coming? I'm so looking forward to meeting her."

Every time there'd been a lull in the activity at the station, he called, only to get Claire's voice mail. Worry fueled his drive home more than the promise of a few hours' sleep and hot shower. He parked the car and made his way through the downstairs, peeling his outerwear off as he went.

"I'm not sure…" Asking her advice danced on the end of his tongue. Any time he'd turned to her for help, she'd given her input then supported his decision. She was also his go-to parent when it came to relationships, having been the one to give him the box of condoms when he left for college. He wasn't so sure she'd understand the hot mess that was now his love life.

"What's going on that you're not telling me?" she asked, her voice at once sounding concerned and teasing. "You and Max aren't letting a girl come between you, are you?"

Sean clenched his eyelids. Boy, had they let Claire get between them, but that wasn't the half of it. If he didn't know what to do with his feelings for his best friend, it seemed the confusion went doubly for Max. Sean couldn't take another night of the three of them avoiding each other. He'd get things out in the open, one way or the other, if only he knew how to go about it.

"What's the saying?" she asked interrupting his thoughts. "Bros before…"

"Mom," he pleaded. "Where do you hear this stuff?"

She laughed. "I keep up. Try to put aside whatever romantic drama you three have got going on for a couple hours. I've planned a wonderful evening and I want everyone to have a great time."

"I'll do my best." Seeing Max on his way down the stairs, Sean needed to end the conversation before his friend slipped away. "See you soon, Mom."

Max passed him on the stairs without speaking.

"Hold up," Sean demanded, his temper burning through the fatigue.

"I'm in a hurry," Max said without missing a step.

Seeing his friend's black gym bag, Sean asked. "Did they start requiring appointments down at Twenty-Four Hour Fitness?"

"Fine," he growled, setting down the bag. "What is it?"

Sean ached to touch his friend. "Mom wanted to let you know she's order those quiches you like."

The hard lines of Max's face softened. "Tell her thanks, but I'm not going."

"Come on," Sean said, gripping Max's shoulder. "What happened the other night doesn't have to change our friendship." When he wouldn't make eye contact, Sean wondered if something had changed. "This is more than us kissing. What happened?"

The muscle in Max's jaw ticked. "I fucked Claire."

Anger lanced through Sean. "You said you were stepping back. Was that a lie?"

"No." Max looked to the living room below. "I came home last night and she was over there watching T.V. I started off telling her she needed to either give you a chance or leave you alone altogether. She'd seen the news report about the woman who's been murdered and was freaked out." He shook his head. "The rest just happened."

Sean drew in a steadying breath. "So are you going to make a play for her?" he asked, not certain what he'd do if Max said he wanted her for himself.

"No. It was a one-time only thing." Max made eye contact. "I made it clear I wasn't interested in starting something with her. Besides, it's you she wants."

"I'm not so sure," Sean said. Despite the phone sex, Claire didn't seem any closer to changing her mind about him. "What about me?" he asked, figuring he might as well get everything out in the open. "Are you interested in starting something with me?"

"No." Max started down the stairs.

"Why? You were into that kiss. I could tell."

He shrugged. "So what if I was. You're hot, and I had a weak moment. I've screwed things up with one friend. I won't risk that with you."

"Nice choice of words." Sean's anger flared. "So you'll fuck anybody else but me."

"Just leave it. Okay." Max made a U-turn, leaving the gym bag on the landing as if it were too heavy to carry when paired with the burden of guilt. "I'll go to your parents' thing tonight, but back off on the other stuff."

This wasn't over, by half. Sean was tired of playing the good guy, the one who let the people around him call the shots. Claire felt something for him; he knew it in his gut. Max wanted this thing between them to happen, too. He'd handle her when she got home from work. Right now he had a best friend who needed a kick in the ass.

Ass indeed.

Sean opened the door to the hall bathroom in time to get a good look at Max's perfect backside as he stepped into the shower. A tattoo of a broadsword started at his nape and ran down his muscular back.

He glared over his shoulder at Sean. "I said we were done."

"The hell we are. You're not the only bossy one in the house." He stripped out of his uniform and joined his friend in the shower. "If you can fuck Claire and call it a one-off, I want my turn."

He gripped Max's nape, pulling him in for a brutal kiss. Their tongues warred, but where Sean had given over the lead before, this time he held his own. When he'd made his point, he gentled his kisses, trailing them across Max's whiskered jaw.

"God," Max groaned as he angled his head, giving Sean access to his neck.

The woodsy scent of his body wash mixed with his natural scent and filled Sean's head. He nibbled his way across his friend's shoulder, tasting the saltiness of dried perspiration. "I thought you were headed to the gym."

Max raked his fingers through Sean's hair, tilting his chin. "I was hoping to avoid telling you what a shitty friend I am."

"We'll deal with that later." He snaked an arm around Max's middle, pulling him in close. Their cocks brushed, as Sean worked his erection against his friend's.

Reaching between their bodies, Sean cupped Max's sack. "Don't deny me this." He stroked Max's hard length from root to tip. Then he dropped to his knees and took Max into his mouth.

He ran his tongue around the ridge, paying special attention to the V on the underside. Going on nothing more than what he found pleasurable about oral sex, he switched between running his tongue along the thickly veined shaft and deep draws to the back of his throat. Max's cock lengthened and his head flared, making it impossible for Sean to take him all. Backing off, he turned his attention to the slit at the tip.

"Shit," Max hissed as a burst of pre-cum filled Sean's mouth. "I'm going to unload if you don't stop."

Sean grinned. "That's the general idea."

Cupping his face, Max said, "Not this time."

"Then at least let me get you off." After standing, he reached for the body wash. When he'd poured some into his palm, he stroked it along Max's cock. "I want to show you how good this can be between us."

Max clenched his jaw but said nothing as Sean worked his erection. Then gripping Sean's nape with one hand, Max began stroking him with the other. As many times as Sean had gotten himself off, nothing compared to the feel of his best friend's rough fingers working over his shaft.

He gave into the primal urge, pumping his hips until his balls drew tight against his body. "I'm so close." He growled, trying to keep at bay the boiling orgasm until he'd gotten Max off.

Max stilled Sean's hand. "This time is for you." With that he dropped to his knees and sucked Sean's cock so hard he practically syphoned the orgasm from him. By the time Max finished, Sean's legs felt like spaghetti.

As amazing as that had been, he wanted more. He wanted what his friend had so freely given Claire. "Fuck me."

Max stood. "You're not ready," he said, stilling Sean's hands when he again reached for Max's cock.

Sean's anger flared. After what he'd just done, how could Max say he wasn't ready? "You don't get to decide that."

"Okay, then. I'm not ready."

He brushed his thumb across Sean's lips, making him strongly consider begging.

"Since David and Lydia, sex has been no more than random hook-ups. It wasn't like that with the three of us the other night. Sex would mean so much more with you."

God he was right. Sean nodded, putting some space

between them. "I understand. I don't like it, but I understand."

"So, are we good?"

"Yeah." Not everything had been cleared up. Sean still wanted to see where Claire fit into the picture, but some of the weight was off his shoulders. That might have had something to do with the orgasm he'd had, but it felt damned good to have recovered some of their easy friendship. "I'm starving." He reached for a towel, passing one to Max.

He slung an arm around Sean's shoulders. "Good. Let's order a pizza and catch a fight on cable while we wait for Claire."

"Will you help me if she tries to back out of going to my folks' house?" he asked, knotting the towel at his hips.

"Sure," Max said, squeezing Sean's shoulder as they stepped into the hall. "I'll also help you find out what's keeping her from saying 'yes' to you." He met Sean's gaze. "And don't worry. When the time comes, I won't get in your way."

Not the answer he wanted. Deep in his soul, he knew there was a way for the three of them to be happy together. "It doesn't have to be an either/or thing," he said as he entered his room for a fresh change of clothes.

The two of them passed the time with food, a couple beers, and a strategy session on how return their girl to their little kinky trio.

Chapter Eight

Claire boarded the bus, thankful for the heat it provided. At a bone-chilling ten degrees outside, her wool pea coat provided little more than minor resistance against frostbite. According to the weatherman, temperatures that weekend were predicted to be in negative numbers, not that she'd be there to worry about that. Across town, her new identity papers waited for her in the postal box.

As she made her way up the aisle, she ran through the list of things she needed to do before heading home—run by the bakery, pack a few clothes in her backpack—mundane tasks she needed to finish before she and Max joined Sean for his family's Christmas party.

She'd already written the letter to the guys and stowed it in the purse on her lap. They'd likely never forgive her for disappearing without saying goodbye, but at least they'd be around to be angry with her.

So caught up in her own thoughts, she failed to notice her coworker, Zoe, until she sat next to her on the seat.

"This isn't your usual bus," the bubbly brunette said.

Claire shrugged. "I'm running some errands." She hoped she wouldn't be expected to hold up her end of a conversation, since she couldn't focus on anything except how hard it was going to be to leave her two roommates.

"I don't think I stopped running all day," Zoe said, laying her head against the seatback. Several seconds passed where neither girl spoke. Then Zoe suddenly jerked her face toward Claire. "Did you ever find out who that guy was who was looking for you?"

Despite her pulse soaring into triple digits, Claire kept her answer neutral. "Must have been a classmate."

"He came looking for you again yesterday, but you were off."

Claire's stomach twisted thinking how close she might have come to seeing Billy face to face. If it was him. "Did you get a look at him this time?" she asked, grasping for something which would allow her to stay.

"I did. He stood around six feet tall and had medium brown hair."

That described half the male population. "So nothing stood out?" Claire asked.

Zoe lifted her gaze in thought. "Yeah, something did. He had really weird eyes."

Fear pricked her scalp. Wide blue eyes played a prominent role in her nightmares. "Weird how?" Claire fought to keep her voice calm.

"I don't know how to explain it," Zoe said shaking her head. "They just creeped me out."

"Good thing he didn't find me then," she said, trying her best to sound disinterested. "So what are your plans for the evening?"

That question was all Zoe needed. She was off and running. "You won't believe who I've got a date with." Claire didn't need to participate in the conversation any further other than nodding. Five minutes later when Zoe came up for a breath, Claire said, "This is my stop."

"Okay," Zoe said. "Have a good night."

"Thanks," she answered. Her throat tightened. "Take care of yourself, Zoe."

She needed to do a better job of controlling her emotions. If she was going to get teary-eyed saying good-bye to a coworker, what would she be like when she walked away from Max and Sean?

She braced herself against the gusting wind as she hit the sidewalk. Then she melted into a crowd of people headed up the street. Five blocks later, she was inside the postal store. She didn't visit her mailbox with any regularity. No need to since she rarely communicated with the people from her past. But she'd gotten an email last night telling her to expect to find her new documents. She shoved the key into the lock, anticipation making her hands shake. There it was in a business-sized envelope, her new identity. She let her backpack slide off her shoulder and tore off the end of the envelope. Out slid several plastic cards. Her eyes zeroed in on the bottom of her new bankcard. Shawna Maxwell. It was stupid, sentimental, and she didn't look anything like a Shawna. She was in love with both her guys and taking a name that reminded her of them seemed like a good idea at the time.

After memorizing the information she could glean from the new bankcard, she flipped to her driver's license. Mr. Blackwell was not only brilliant at creating a new person out of thin air, he wasn't too bad with Photoshop. He'd altered the photo she'd sent, making her a redhead with blue eyes. She'd have to get it cut into a shoulder length bob to match the picture, but at least she could quit wearing the colored lenses that darkened her blue-green eyes.

Tucking the new cards into the outer pocket of her backpack, she hoped this would be the last time she had to run from Billy. The money her father scraped together for her was nearly gone. After paying Mr. Blackwell, she had barely enough for a bus ticket out of town, so she'd have to find a job in Seattle quickly.

Her new identity came with a non-descript history fitting a twenty-two-year-old graduate with a degree in accounting. In real life, she'd be twenty-five in May and had been working on a degree in Musical Performance at Bryant College.

Having collected the envelope, she raced up the street to catch the bus that would take her home. An hour later, she arrived at her doorstep. Now all she had to do was to fake her way through the next few hours. She'd barely gotten a foot inside when her acting skills were tested.

"You took a really long time getting home," Sean said, his brow furrowed.

Guilt lanced through her. Would he still feel as protective toward her if he knew what she'd done with Max? "I finally found a bakery that carried a cake I wanted to bring to your folks tonight. It was all the way across town."

A wide grin creased his face. "You're still going?"

"If that's okay."

He brushed back a lock of her hair, a gesture that made her heart ache with its tenderness. "It's more than okay."

She stepped out of his reach. "I need a quick shower, and I'll be ready to go."

Before she could get away, Sean snagged her hand.

"Claire, it's okay." His voice was low and soft as if he were speaking to a frightened animal. "Max told me what happened."

She clenched her eyelids. *God, why had he done that?* There was no point in hurting Sean. Claire and Max both understood there could be nothing more between them. She checked it with his expression— only sweet concern shown back in his gorgeous green eyes. "You're not mad?"

"I was." He shrugged. "But I can appreciate his appeal." His hand skimmed along her collar bone. "And yours."

"I'm sorry," she said. "I've made a mess out of things." And now she was leaving. "I want to make things right with you both."

He kissed the top of her head. "We can talk later." He pointed to the pink bakery box on the kitchen table. "Tell me about this cake. It's not one of those awful fruit cakes is it?"

She smiled. "It's a King Cake. It's for after Christmas. It ushers in Carnival." A smile tugged at her lips as she remembered how her family celebrated the days leading up to Mardi Gras. "I'll tell you about it later. I have to take a shower, and then get changed for your folks' party."

****

Max stuck his head out of his room in time to see Claire shut herself inside the bathroom. *Nice.* He probably had a good fifteen minutes before she emerged, plenty of time to search her room for clues as to why his once light-hearted roommate was jumping at shadows. With a backward glance toward the bathroom, he slipped inside.

Once there he did a quick scan of the small room. Atop her twin bed lay a red wrap-style dress. He'd seen it on her before and knew he and Sean would have a devil of a time keeping their hands to themselves at the party later. The dress and a pair of boots were the only items out of place. Their girl was such a neat freak that he'd have to be careful to leave her things where he found them. Suddenly the door opened, catching Max with his hands inside her dresser.

"What the fuck are you doing?"

Max jumped at the sound of his friend's voice, but kept up his careful search. "What does it look like?"

"She's going to hurt you and make it look like an accident."

"Only if she finds out." Max shot Sean a glare. "Which she won't because you're going to keep a look out."

"This doesn't set well with me," he said, his arms folded across his chest.

"Duly noted."

Sean's gaze darted around the room. "What are you after?"

"I'm not sure," Max said, taking up where he'd left off his search. He eased the top drawer closed and opened another. "I'll know when I find it." He voiced what he'd been thinking ever since he'd startled her the other night as she slept on the sofa. "Something's up, and I intend to find out what it is."

"You noticed that, too? I thought it was because of the three of us fooling around."

Max shrugged. "That's probably part of it, but there's more."

"So where do you want me to start looking?"

He jerked his head toward Claire's desk. "Check out her email and see if she's gotten anything that might have frightened her. She's been really jumpy lately."

Sean opened the lid of her laptop and tapped his fingers over the keys. "And grumpy," he added. "I hope we haven't screwed things up with her."

"You haven't." When he found no clues in her dresser, he turned his attention to her closet. For a girl who worked retail, Claire had few clothes. Then again, she didn't have much of anything. The top of her dresser held a small jewelry box and a bottle of perfume. Otherwise, there were no decorations, no clues to the past she alluded to the other night.

After finishing his search of her closet, he moved to the side of her bed. A sense of urgency sped his movements as he peeked inside the top drawer of her nightstand. Seeing inside, the corner of his mouth turned up. The toys and lube were the first thing he'd come across that held any clue to who she was outside of a young twenty-year-old who liked dangly earrings and high heeled shoes. Sweetness also liked to play.

He stowed that info for later thought. At best, he had another three or four minutes before Claire came in and made good on Sean's prediction. What he was doing was wrong on a number of levels, but there wasn't anything he wouldn't do to help her, even if he had to risk incurring her wrath.

Max went for the bottom drawer. "Check it," he said, holding up one of three boxes of hair color. "Seems our girl isn't exactly what she seems to be." She also had a stash of colored contact lenses.

"So," Sean said, shrugging. "Lots of girls dye their hair."

"True." Alone, the facts they'd uncovered meant little. Combined, they screamed of someone who was hiding something. Before Max could share his thoughts or search under her bed, the sound of water stopped.

Sean closed the lid on her laptop. "We need to get out of here."

Max caught his friend before he opened the door. Speaking barely above a whisper he explained, "Tonight after we get back from your folks', I want you to distract her while I make a better search." He still needed to check under her bed and inside her backpack.

Sean's brow furrowed. "Why don't we just come out and ask her what's wrong?"

Before Sean's family took Max in, his home life was a textbook case of alcohol and abuse. As a result, lying became second nature, especially when it came to hiding his family's shameful secrets. His gut told him she utilized the same defensive tactic. "I don't think she'd tell us the truth."

"Then shouldn't we respect her privacy?" Sean, the voice of reason asked, his arms folded across his chest.

If this was a matter of Claire having something in her past she'd rather not share, even if it was past brushes with the law, it would be different. "Not when she's in danger, no."

Sean's eyes widened. "What makes you think…?"

Max arched an eyebrow. Given what he'd experienced as a kid, further explanation was unnecessary.

"Okay, I'll help. But what should I do with her?"

Max rolled his eyes. Despite years of his corrupting influence, Sean was still such a Boy Scout. "What do you think you could do with a beautiful girl that would keep her occupied for say an hour or so?"

A slow smile formed on Sean's lips. "Fuck yeah. I'll be your diversion any day."

****

After leaving her room, Sean hesitated at the doorway of his own. The guilt he felt at spying on her warred with his conviction that Max was right.

"Claire," he called when she stepped out of the bathroom.

She waved a hand and kept walking. "I know. I'm making us late."

"It's not that." He motioned for her. "I want to talk for a second."

She drew the terry cloth robe tighter around her. "I don't have time."

He closed the distance between them. "You've got thirty seconds for me to see how you're doing." He breathed in her peppermint scented body wash and the image of him licking her body like she was an erotic candy cane popped in his head. "Are you okay? You seem distracted this past week." Sean gave into his imagination's urging and kissed her neck. "I've missed you," he confessed, letting his hands slip beneath the folds of her robe.

He cupped her breast, tweaking her nipple between his thumb and finger. Outside of one very hot session of phone sex, they'd only been together that once. As his arm banded her slender waist, it felt as if he'd known her body for longer. He knew that suckling her breast would make her moan, and that trailing kisses up her thigh elicited shudders of desire. He wanted to know what hid behind her chocolate brown eyes more than anything, and that was saying something considering his dick pulsed with every heartbeat. "Won't you tell me what's going on? I know if you tell me, I can help."

Her face still buried in the crook of his neck, she shook her head. "It's nothing."

Sean tilted her chin. The warm hue of her eyes spoke to him. They also made him wonder at their real color. "I know you're lying."

Claire narrowed her eyes. "I'm working retail at Christmas, and I have two pushy roommates. That's my problem." A few tears shimmered in her eyes. "It doesn't matter," she said, turning her face. "In a few days it will all be better."

With that, she pushed out of his embrace and stormed into her room. The sound of her door slamming echoed. Now he was convinced Max was right, and the veiled promise she'd left him with twisted his gut. With a backward glance, he headed to Max's room ready to help him hatch a plot to uncover what secrets Claire was hiding from them. He had another equally complicated problem to solve—getting Max to make love to him.

Chapter Nine

"Rich people do *not* know how to decorate their houses for Christmas," Claire announced from the rear seat of Sean's car. As the trio made their way to his family home in the Chicago suburb of Lake Forest, the outdoor displays diminished inversely to the size and cost of the houses.

Both men laughed at her latest commentary. With the hours she had to spend with them growing short, she made up her mind to savor every moment. Making Sean and Max laugh ranked high on her list of pleasures.

"What have you got against tasteful and understated?" Max asked from the shotgun position next to Sean.

Claire gave herself a mental pat on the back for orchestrating the seating arrangement, which put the best friends next to each other. From her position in the rear, she witnessed the furtive glances pinging back and forth between them.

"I have nothing against either, except when it comes to Christmas decorations." She watched as house after house bore little more than candles in the windows and large wreaths on front doors. Back home in Maryville, bigger and brighter was the norm, and outdoor displays were a source of family pride.

All her mirth dried up as Sean pulled into the

driveway in front of a house that was easily three times the size of her family's home. Her gaze traveled from the steeply pitched slate roof down to the half-timber framing and leaded-glass windows of the Tudor-style mansion.

"This place is huge," she whispered to Max as he held the car door open for her. Her mother would be three shades of green seeing the Dalton's home.

"Tell me about it," he said, taking from her the armload of toys they were donating to Safe House as part of the fund raising party. "I got lost trying to find the bathroom the first time Sean invited me over."

Sean joined them at the front of his car. "Don't let the size intimidate you. As my mom always says, we put our pants on one leg at a time same as everyone else," he said wrapping an arm around her and guiding her between two luxury cars.

"Yeah, but from the looks of things, those pants cost a hundred dollars a pop."

With her in the middle, they took the luminary-lined walkway to an arched front door. Her stomach did flip-flops as Sean reached for the wrought iron door handle.

As if he sensed her anxiety, Max gripped her hand. "Don't worry. The Dalton's are good people. If they can accept a juvenile delinquent like me, they'll accept your sweet self with open arms."

Not if they knew she had slept with both Sean and Max. Regardless of how the Daltons had opened their home to Max, they'd never accept their son being involved in a ménage relationship. She brushed away that concern. It was one she'd never have to contend with again, as long as they kept their hands to themselves for the next few hours.

Sean was helping her out of her coat when a smartly dressed woman entered the huge foyer. Her face lit up in a smile reminiscent of Sean's. "Get in here and give me a hug," she said opening her arms.

Both men obeyed, taking turns gently embracing the slender woman.

With a mile-wide grin, Sean gestured toward Claire. "Mom, this is Claire Matthews."

She extended her hand to Sean's mother. "Pleased to meet you. You have a very lovely home."

"Thank you, and please call me Olivia," Mrs. Dalton replied, through a polite smile. Her gaze assessed Claire from head to toe in an instant. "Sean's told me so much about you."

Though Claire cut her eyes at him, he only shrugged and tugged her deeper into the house. "Come on, I want you to meet the rest of my family."

With his hand at the small of her back, he led her past a spruce pine decorated with white lights and hundreds of painted glass ornaments. Beneath the tree were dozens of brightly wrapped presents for the kids at Safe House. As she brushed past one of the tree's branches, the crisp scent brought back memories of her childhood, adding homesickness to the list of emotions warring for space in her heart.

A group of twenty or so people milled around a large family room where a rock fireplace dominated the two-story room. The large scale of the room added to the sense she'd traveled too far from her south Alabama roots. Instead of giving into country-mouse-come-to-the-city feelings, she fixed a well-practiced smile on her lips as Sean introduced her to his family and the other guests. Some were people she recognized from Sean and Max's work, and others she'd seen featured in the Lifestyle section of the newspaper.

She was only half listening to Mr. Dalton sharing his youngest daughter, Meghan's brilliant performance in *The Nutcracker* when Max joined them. He pressed a kiss to her temple before placing a cup in her hand. "I thought you might enjoy something to warm you up."

"Thanks," she murmured, hoping no one noticed the kiss or that Sean had threaded his fingers through hers.

She brought the cup to her lips, breathing in the spices before letting the wassail dance over her tongue. Christmas had always been her favorite holiday, partly because it seemed to involve every sense the way no other could. Taking in the warm luxury of the Dalton home, her thoughts traveled to what lay ahead for her. Unlike her mother, Claire never aspired to wealth. A sense of belonging meant far more to her. With Sean and Max flanking her, she wondered if perhaps one day, she'd have run far enough from Billy that she could put down roots—maybe even have a family of her own.

"Have you ever danced," Sean's father asked, drawing her to the here and now.

It took a moment for the question to register. "No, sir," she answered, chasing melancholy thoughts from her mind. Though as the accompanist for Maryville Dance Company, she'd seen the ballet countless times.

"I'm surprised," Mrs. Dalton said, coming to join them. "You're obviously a head turner."

Claire tugged her hand from Sean's. "Thank you, ma'am," she responded, unsure whether to take the compliment at face value or read more into the comment.

She studied Sean's mother from the corner of her eye. In her late forties and with the subtle grooming of the well-to-do, Mrs. Dalton played the perfect hostess with enough ease and style to give any Alabama belle a run for her money.

The similarities caused Claire's self-preservation instincts to kick in. After Billy was sent away to the psychiatric hospital, the story of her rape and attack didn't die down. A coven of perfectly groomed, beautifully mannered women kept the story fresh in everyone's mind. Despite the fact it was she who bore the scars, Billy and the entire Townsend clan were painted as the victims. So she had reason to be suspicious of women who could wield, "bless your heart," and "lying tramps aren't welcome in my home," with the same cutting effect.

While Mr. Dalton moved on to talk about the accomplishments of his other children, Mrs. Dalton touched Claire lightly on the arm. "Dear, I hate to pull you away from the party, but would you mind helping me in the kitchen for a moment?"

Claire would have rather crawled across glass than be lured into a secluded corner with this woman, but good manners trumped self-defense. "Certainly," she said, following the woman out of the room.

Cabinets of warm wood, marble countertops and shiny stainless appliances dominated the kitchen. "What can I do to help?" she asked, despite knowing Mrs. Dalton didn't need Claire's help pulling dinner together. Especially as servers from a catering company were busy filling trays of appetizers and a white-jacketed chef was manning the large cooktop.

Stepping across the marble floor in her high heels, Mrs. Dalton pulled out a chair at a round table in the corner of the kitchen. Then she gestured for Claire to do the same. After she'd taken the seat next to Mrs. Dalton, she braced herself for whatever the woman was about to dish out.

"You'll excuse the ruse, my dear," she began sweetly. "I simply wanted to have a moment so the two of us could have a private talk."

Claire schooled her face in to a well-practiced mask. "All right."

"I'm sure you've seen by now how close Sean and Max are."

She managed a nod in response to Mrs. Dalton's beginning salvo.

"It's also equally apparent to anyone with eyes both of my boys have it bad for you." She gripped Claire's hand. "I'm pleading with you not to do anything to tear those two apart."

Where Claire had prepared to hear an accusation or a thinly veiled threat, she hadn't expected this heart-felt plea. It cut her to the quick. With the same surety that she knew she was blameless in the events surrounding her rape, she was equally certain of the guilt she bore for any fissures in Sean and Max's relationship. "I won't; that's a promise," she said, meeting Mrs. Dalton's eye.

"That's good to hear," Mrs. Dalton said, patting Claire's hand. All the tension eased from the woman's body. "You'll have to forgive the mother lion routine, but both my boys mean the world to me."

Claire smiled inwardly. Mrs. Dalton's

straightforward tactic little resembled the ferocity she'd experienced in the past. It also made her envious. At one point in her life, she too had been cossetted by a loving family, but that all changed after her attack.

"They're important to me, too," she said, feeling closer to her guys than she had to anyone in years. "I won't do anything to come between them." In fact, she intended to play an active role in getting the two of them together.

"Very good then," Mrs. Dalton said with a nod. "If you'll take that tray of appetizers, we'll rejoin the others."

Claire did as she was instructed, placing a silver tray on one of the small tables dotting the family room but didn't rejoin the party. Instead, she hovered at the room's entry. Sean's hand rested against Max's shoulder in such a casual way that had she not known of their feelings for one another she'd have missed the significance of it. She hoped as she slipped from the room, that if the two of them got together, the Dalton family would embrace the couple.

Claire wandered through the public rooms of the home's lower level, looking for a quiet corner to hide in until dinnertime. Her pensive mood made her poor company at such a merry party. She stuck her head in the formal dining room, to find two uniformed caterers busy setting the table with Lenox Christmas dishes.

If the multi-million-dollar house, heirloom antiques, and magazine-worthy kitchen didn't send her mother over an envious ledge, the display of china, silver, and glassware would. Sarah Matthews considered herself of higher station than she'd married into and worked to create an illusion of style and southern grace that her husband's wallet couldn't quite pull off.

Claire's father had been able to provide something more important, at least to Claire. From the time she could climb onto a piano bench, she'd taken lessons. As she drifted into the formal living room, her heart ached with longing. An ebony grand piano dominated the space. Claire gravitated to it, easing open the lid to the keyboard. The instrument she'd spent hours playing was a second-hand upright her father traded for a rebuilt '60's muscle car.

Time compressed and she was back in the First Methodist church, playing the opening notes of "Jesu, Joy of Man's Desiring." The music broke past the barrier of her past where she'd kept it and a thousand other memories.

She'd held such optimistic beliefs then. That if she practiced long enough, she'd make her way to Carnegie Hall. She also believed that a handsome man with money and prestige in the community would stop when she told him, "no."

"I didn't know you could play," Sean murmured as he slid beside her on the bench.

Her breath caught at the unexpected intrusion into her thoughts. "I can't," she said, closing the lid and tucking her hands in her lap. "It's just something I memorized when I was younger."

From behind her Mrs. Dalton said, "It was beautiful. Would you play something else? A Christmas carol, perhaps."

Claire turned to see a dozen or so of the guests had gathered. "I don't…" Her words stuck in her throat. The feel of the keys under her fingers and the clear sound of the notes brought out too many memories.

"There's some sheet music in the bench," Mrs. Dalton offered, her smile more genuine than before.

Max moved to stand on the other side of her. "You don't have to if you don't want to."

She shook her head when she most wanted to wrap herself in his broad body. He seemed to see through the façade she created, something she'd have to be cognizant of if she planned to slip out of their home tonight without a confrontation. "I don't mind," she said, standing. She opened the lid and retrieved several sheets of music from the bench. "As long as you don't mind my clunkers."

The next hour flew past as she led the family and their guests in dozens of songs. When she finished a particularly allegro "Carol of the Bells", the room broke out in laughter and thunderous applause. Through the dinner that followed and the ride back home, Claire's brain was clouded with the myriad of conflicting emotions. After their tête-à-tête, Mrs. Dalton went out of her way to shower Claire with kindness, making her feel guilty and happy in equal measure. Especially as she watched Sean and Max, who couldn't keep their eyes off one another.

****

From the driver's seat, Sean looked over his shoulder at Claire. She hadn't said two words since the three of them left his parents' house. Instead, she'd gazed out the window, her thoughts seemingly far from the Chicago suburbs.

"We're home, sweetness," Max said, killing the car's engine.

She blinked a couple times before answering.

"Sorry. I guess my mind was off at the North Pole."

Somehow, Sean didn't think her thoughts had taken her to some fantasy land; he noted the sadness in her eyes. He wrapped an arm around her shoulders as the three of them made their way inside. "I hope you had a good time tonight. My parents really like you."

"I did, thank you," she said shucking her coat and shoes by the back door. Then over her shoulder she added, "You have a great family."

She crossed the kitchen with purpose, but Max quickly cut off her path into the living room. "Where you headed?" he asked. "It's still early."

"I'm going to turn in," she said, plastering on her face one of those pretend smiles he had seen so much of lately. "I'll see you later."

"Hold up a minute," Max said, snagging her arm. Over her head, he eyed Sean. While the family had been occupied with Claire's playing, they'd snuck off for a few minutes. The plan was for Sean to lure Claire into his bed while Max finished reconnoitering Claire's room.

During the quick meeting they'd had in Max's old room, Sean's mind had strayed from the topic. It had taken everything in him to keep his hands off Max. It should have felt strange to bridge the gap between friends to lovers, especially since Sean had never been attracted to another guy.

Instead, kissing Max felt more right than anything he'd ever done—with the exception of making love to Claire. He still wasn't sure how'd it work between the three of them, but despite Max's reservations, Sean knew it would.

"I think Sean has a present he wants to give you."

Sean nodded when Max jerked his chin toward the stairs. What his friend didn't know was that Sean had altered the game plan to include Max in the tryst. Manipulation didn't come naturally to Sean, but if he ever planned to get either of the people he loved back into bed, he was going to have to learn. And quickly.

Taking Claire's free hand, Sean slid the other around Maxi's broad shoulders. "Actually it's a gift from both of us."

Understanding flared in Claire's eyes. "I like presents."

Max poked Sean in the ribs but instead of letting go, Sean slid his palm up to grip Max's nape. Then Sean took another bold step, one he hoped would enflame the passion simmering beneath Max's taciturn exterior. Sean licked his lips while holding his best friend's gaze.

Payoff. Max's nostrils flared, even as he growled his dissatisfaction at Sean veering off plan.

Claire broke the stalemate between the two. "I guess Christmas really is the time for wishes to come true." Her hand joined his in caressing Max. "I want each of you to make love to me." She ducked her chin. "At the same time."

Chapter Ten

Max groaned inwardly. As hard as it had been to refuse Sean's advances earlier in the evening, saying "no" to Claire was impossible. Especially with the gift she offered. "Are you sure?"

A smile played on her lips as she batted her eyelashes. "Yes, Sir."

Holy fuck. Did she have any idea what that did to him?

"Girlfriend, you are playing with fire," Sean warned, though he was smiling as he shook his head like he couldn't wait to see how this all played out.

Fire indeed. Although it was Max who was most likely to get burned. Those two words, slipping between those two luscious lips, and from the sweetest girl he'd ever known, and any thoughts of walking away from her evaporated.

"Don't stop her," he said, stalking over to her. "I like it when she calls me 'Sir.'" Visions of her tied to his bed overwrote the earlier plan.

"Sweet," Sean said, pulling both Max and Claire across the living room.

The three of them stumbled up the stairs, sharing kisses and caresses that had Max panting. "Sean's room," he said, tugging his lovers down the hallway.

Once they were in the room that featured a California king with at least a dozen pillows on it, he started undressing. Midway through stepping out of his pants, Sean caught Max's attention as he reached over his head to tug off his shirt one-handed.

God, my boy has some abs on him. The arrow of hair that began at his navel drew Max's eye to the tent at the front of Sean's pants.

The only thing which could possibly divert Max's attention from his best friend's washboard abs and bulging cock, was the sight of Claire's ivory skin. With the pull of a string, she unwrapped herself from her red dress just like a package on Christmas morning.

She turned her back to them, flashing her ass covered only by a strip of lace at the top of her hips. Placing her palms on the end of Sean's bed she said, "I want you to spank me, Max."

Sean froze with his black dress pants halfway down his muscular legs. "What the…"

Claire taunted them with a shimmy of her hips. "For fun, Sean. I've read about it in some of the erotic romances I've downloaded. I want to see if it's as hot as they make it out to be."

Okay, sure there was the tiniest part of him that wondered what had suddenly come over her since she'd spent the past few days keeping him and Sean at arm's length. However, the biggest part of Max's brain—both of them—wanted to see Claire's ass a rosy shade of pink. He sidled up to her, letting his hand trail over her back. "Don't you just love e-books?" He caressed her pert backside.

He brought his hand down on her ass in a quick swat meant to awaken the nerve endings. When her head lolled back on her shoulders, he delivered two more in quick succession. The groan that escaped her lips was as sweet as the music she'd played earlier because it meant he was the instrument that brought her pleasure. He covered the pink places where he'd swatted her with his hand, letting the heat sink in. When he sensed she was ready, he delivered two more, one to each cheek.

While Max had been lighting up Claire's ass, Sean had played witness. His hands fisted by his side, he seemed ready to intervene at the first sign this wasn't what she wanted. "Holy cow." Sean breathed. "She's really into this." He took a step closer to the bed.

Max cut his eyes to his buddy. "Would I be doing this if she wasn't?"

"No," he said, "but I never imagined our girl was so kinky."

There were a lot of things they didn't know about her. As much as he was into what they were doing, Max hadn't completely abandoned the plan he and Sean made. They'd get her good and sated, then he'd finish his search of her room.

By the sixth time his palm met with the tender flesh, he figured she'd had enough. Her breath came in shallow pants and her legs were quivering, but her head was loose on her shoulders. He'd never seen someone reach sub space so quickly, but as a novice, he didn't want to push her. "Let's get her up on the bed."

Sean pulled back the comforter, and then helped Max ease her onto her back. In a flash, his buddy was on the bed next to her. Propped on one elbow, he trailed his hand over her belly. When his hand dipped just below her navel, he shot Max a glance. The question of where Claire got her scar had to be on Sean's mind as much as it was on his.

"Give those luscious tits of hers some loving, Seany-boy," Max instructed. He wanted to taste her pussy that by now had to be juicy and sweet like a ripe peach.

He pressed his palms against her inner thighs, bringing her cunt into view. Beautifully bare, her outer lips were pink and when he opened her, he found her core creamy. He brought his mouth to her clit, drawing the bundle of nerves between his lips. When Claire moaned, he pumped a finger inside her core. She was so wet his fingers slid into her channel with ease. And tight. God, his cock ached for wanting to feel her squeeze him.

In a matter of seconds, an orgasm exploded through her. Her center gripped his fingers as she worked her clit against his face. He could spend hours going down on her and never grow tired of the experience. When she came back into herself, she pushed her hair out of her face, revealing eyes glassy and a little unfocused. "Have you had enough, little one?"

"No." She shook her head as she turned her attention to Sean. Wrapping her arms around his neck, she kissed him down to the bed. Then she straddled his hips.

"Give me a hand," Sean said, peeking around Claire who had his arms pinned over his head. The guy sported a broad smile that let him know, his boy loved letting Claire have her way with him. His cock tented his boxer briefs, making Max's mouth water. The only experience to rival going down on Claire was giving Sean head.

Max's hand shook as he made contact with the skin

above the waistband of Sean's underwear. Drawing the material over his erection required a little finesse and had Max's cock standing at attention.

Claire rose on her knees then inched her hips backward, making clear what she wanted. Max gripped Sean's erection, and rolled on a condom. He then squirted a generous amount of lube. Unable to resist feeling the firm length in his palm, Max pumped his fist over the velvet-covered steel a couple times before offering it up to Claire's waiting cunt.

Max held Claire's hips as she took Sean in to the root.

She hummed. "God, that's so, so good."

As big as Sean was—as they both were—Max wondered if she might reconsider trying double penetration. If so, he'd let her have her fill with Sean and then if she still wanted, he'd make love to her ass.

"Please," she said, looking over her shoulder before she lowered her body to Sean's chest. Max didn't know what kind of romance novels she'd been reading, but someone had been doing their research. He massaged her lower back, letting a finger slip between her twin globes once he had her good and relaxed. The key to anal was relaxation, small steps, and lots of lube.

"I'm going to play back here, sweetness. Tell me to stop if anything scares you or hurts." He waited for her to nod before he pressed a fingertip to her anus. As he teased her tight rosette, Max made contact with Sean's sack. His buddy groaned like the touch was the best thing ever, then opened his legs wider. "I've got my hands full," Max teased as he cupped Sean firmly. "I can only please one of you at a time."

"Later then," came his buddy's breathless

response.

That was a promise Max very much wanted to keep.

For now, he focused to giving Claire her wish. "I want you to push back against my finger," he instructed. When she flowered open, he pushed past the first ring of tight muscle.

"Keep breathing." He stroked his lubed finger deeper into her back channel, moving slowly so as to not cause her pain.

"It burns," she said, tightening on his finger.

He stilled. "Do you want me to stop?"

"No—it feels—." She panted. "It's so good. I want more."

He complied with her request, and as he did, he could feel Sean's cock just on the other side of the thin wall.

"God, that's good." Sean moaned. "You're killing me, Max."

"Think of something else," he ordered. "I'm not rushing her."

"I know," Sean said breathless. "But there are only so many bones in the human body and I've already run through all the baseball stats I know."

Claire reached behind to grip Max's hand. "I'm ready. Just go slow."

He bent down to press a kiss to the small of her back. He'd had dozens of lovers—both male and female. Some had wanted it rough and others had wanted to do things that even surprised him. No one had ever touched him the way she did with her trust. He slipped his finger in all the way, stretching her, and when he felt like she could accommodate him with the least amount of discomfort, he withdrew his finger.

His hands shook as he rolled on a condom. With his cock poised at her rosette, he drew in a deep breath. He'd never made love to an anal virgin, and the honor Claire bestowed on him as the first to make love to her ass had his heart pounding in his chest. He wished he had the words to say what she meant to him, but they seemed to get tangled with worry and uncertainty on the way to his lips. Instead, he brushed her hair away from her shoulder, kissing her on that sweet spot behind her ear.

The three of them groaned as Max's cock breached the second ring of muscle. She was hot and tight and felt so fucking good it brought tears to his eyes. He reined in the urge to pound into her, sliding by increments the way he had with his finger.

He arched over her back, his arms bracketing both his lovers' shoulders. She buried her face in the crook of Sean's neck and when Max pressed deeper, it brought him inches from Sean's face. His buddy had his eyes clenched, head jacked back, and he bore the expression of sweet agony. Then as Max sank all the way home, Sean's eyes sprang open.

"It's like you're stroking me, Max," he said. "Like you're making love to both of us at the same time."

In that moment, Max realized that in offering herself to both men, she'd found a way to bridge the gap between the two friends. The last of his worries melted away. Making love with Claire and Sean was so different from what he'd done with David and Lydia as to render them completely separate acts. He gently tilted her chin to press a kiss of gratitude to her lips. Then he brought his mouth to Sean's taking it in a tangle of tongue and teeth that left them breathless.

Far too soon, Sean broke the kiss. "I'm not going to last. Help me make her come," he said, slipping his hand between his and Claire's body. Max did the same, and only when she screamed out an orgasm, did they give over to their own needs.

Alternating strokes, they took turns pumping into Claire's willing body. Sean went off first and feeling his dick kicking through the thin wall had Max following quickly. He came so hard he saw stars, and exhausted, he collapsed to the side of the bed. When he caught his breath, Max eased Claire between him and Sean. The three of them lay in a tangle of arms and legs for several minutes before Max worked up the energy to head for the bathroom for some much-needed washcloths. When he returned, he and Sean took turns bathing the beautiful temptress between them.

If they were having a grinning contest, it would be a three-way tie whose smile was bigger. "Was it everything you thought it would be, sweetness?" Max asked.

She nodded. "The best present I've had since the Barbie Dream House," she said, stretching her arms over her head.

Max had to agree. If things kept going the way they were, he might learn to love the holidays.

Chapter Eleven

Claire soaked in the secure feeling of lying between two warm bodies. In the weeks to come when loneliness plagued her, she'd pull out this memory. She listened to their breaths and when she was sure Max and Sean were sleeping soundly, she eased out from in between them. As she paused at the foot of the bed to collect her bra and panties, she looked back. Max had gravitated to Sean, his arm slung across Sean's middle.

She crossed the hall to her room, dressed quickly in jeans and a sweatshirt, and pulled a small suitcase from beneath her bed. Then her momentum stalled. She planted her rear on the bed, feeling the weight of emotions slam into her. Her chin fell to her chest as she gave in. The sniveling weak harpy in her head pleaded for her to wake up her roommates and give a full disclosure, including the part where she admitted she was in love with both of them. She'd been through this ring-around-the-rosy and every time came back to the same conclusion. Keeping Sean and Max out of the crap that was her past trumped her selfish desires.

Drawing in a breath, Claire willed herself to her feet. She reached inside her backpack for the letter she'd written. In light of what happened earlier, she needed to add a line. Opening the envelope, she extracted the sheet of pale blue stationery. Tears pooled in her eyes, making the words blurry.

Dear Sean and Max,

By the time you read this, I'll be hours out of town. Max, please don't go all police detective and put out a BOLO on me. I don't want to be found. This has nothing to do with what's gone on between us in the past few days. If anything, it's made leaving that much harder. But it's what's best for all of us. Thank you from the bottom of my heart for everything you've done for me. For opening up your lives to a girl who couldn't return the favor. No one has meant more to me than you two. I love you both.

Claire

Below her signature, she added:

P.S. Promise me that you'll continue to love each other—don't be idiots and pretend you don't. C.M.

Claire propped the envelope against her dresser mirror where they'd find it in the morning when they came looking for her. Then hefting her backpack onto her shoulder, she grabbed her suitcase and opened the bedroom door.

"Going somewhere?" Max asked. His jaw ticked with barely banked anger, sending Claire's pulse into overdrive. When she didn't answer, he kicked off the wall where he'd been waiting. "I asked you a question, little one. I expect an answer."

She hated what she was about to do, but she'd played this scenario in her head enough to know how her guys would react if she told them the truth. Sean would make all kinds of promises about how he could help her. Max would go all dark and dangerous and try to track down Billy. Neither plan would work. Others had done the same and failed, so she was going to have to be cruel to the two men she loved.

"I'm moving out. I told you that the other day."

"You were just going to disappear on us." He glared at her from beneath hooded eyes. "Did you give any thought to what that would do to Sean?"

Claire pointed over her shoulder to her room. "I left you a note explaining everything. I was trying to avoid a confrontation such as this."

Max closed the distance between them, towering over her. "I can't believe you'd do that to him. Have you no idea how much the guy loves you?"

"I've been straight with both of you from the beginning, but neither of you wants to hear that." She fought to get the words past the lump in her throat. "I don't do the relationship thing."

Just then Sean stepped into the hallway, pulling on a pair of sweatpants that hung low on his hips. "What's going on?" He scrubbed his palm over his cropped hair. "Can't this wait till morning?"

Max's glare never left her face. "No, it can't. I just caught Claire trying to sneak away."

In a pair of long-legged strides, Sean joined them. "Why would you do that?"

"On top of that, she's trying to feed me some bullshit line about her disinterest in having a relationship with you."

Pain flashed in Sean's green eyes before he hid it behind a mask of concern. "Claire, baby," he said caressing her cheek with the back of his hand. "We know something's going on, that you're in some kind of trouble. Whatever it is let me…"

"Save you," Claire finished for him.

"Yeah," Sean said.

The venom-laced words burned her throat on the

way out. "I'm going to let you in on something—I don't need saving." She forced herself to hold his gaze. Witnessing the anguish in his green eyes seemed just punishment in light of the pain she caused.

Max threw his arms up and yelled, "Jesus, Claire. What's wrong with you?"

She jerked her face to him, finding it easier to deal with his anger than Sean's concern. "Nothing a few thousand miles won't fix." She broke from Sean's embrace and made for the stairs. But Max was on her before she made two steps.

"That's it," he said, grabbing her wrist. "Sean, get my cuffs off the dresser in my room."

The last thing she saw before he threw her over his shoulder in a fireman's hold was Sean scurrying off to complete his assignment. She struggled to escape. Why was he making this so hard?

"Put me the fuck down, you Neanderthal." She pummeled his back as he carried her down the hall. "I'm not one of your subs you can manhandle any way you choose."

He swatted her ass hard. The heat traveled through her jeans, settling in her pussy. This was so not the time for her body to react to his. She beat against his back, as she struggled to free herself from his grasp. She only succeeded in earning another swat as he continued toward Sean's room.

When he reached Sean's bed, he eased her on to her back with more gentleness than she expected considering how much of a fuss she was continuing to create. He pinned her body to the bed with his, pulling her arms over her head.

"Here you go, Max," Sean said.

Claire struggled, but all she got for her efforts was the sensual feel of Max's hard body atop hers. She stifled the surge of electricity their bodies made. "What do you think you're going to do, cuff me to the bed until I talk?"

"If that's what it takes to get the truth out of you." He snapped a ring to her wrist then attached the other end to the iron bars of Sean's bed.

While she was looking over her head at her arm, he did the same with the other wrist. "Fuck you." Her words came out in a hiss. Then she turned her head away from them so they couldn't see the angry tears pooling in her eyes.

"It's too late for that, sweetness," he murmured low in her ear. "We tried the gentle way, and you wouldn't be straight with us."

Claire pulled on her restraints before giving in and letting her body go limp. Perhaps she could bargain her way out of the situation by offering a version of the truth that would still keep them from getting involved in her mess. "If I promise to tell you why I have to leave, will you un-cuff me?"

Sean eased a hip down to his bed and turned her face toward him. A confident smile played at his lips. "*When* you tell us everything, I'll convince badass here to un-cuff you."

Claire drew in a steadying breath. Not since she'd first given her statement to the police had she said aloud what Billy did to her. Her parents hadn't asked for details, and she'd been too humiliated to offer an explanation to anyone else.

"A little over five years ago, I was home from Bryant College where I was majoring in piano. Billy

Townsend, a boy from my hometown, asked me out on a date. My mom was thrilled since his family owned half the county we lived in. She thought the Townsends were fabulous with their huge antebellum mansion."

Claire clenched her eyelids as the scene played in her head. "Let's just say there's a reason for the saying, 'looks are deceiving.' At the end of the date, Billy expected something in return for his investment of dinner and a movie, and when I refused, he raped me."

The words were no more past her lips than Max bolted into action. "Sean, help me get her out of these." They made quick work of unfastening the cuffs and Max had her wrapped in his arms in seconds. "I'm such an asshole." He buried his face in her hair.

Still in the emotions of reliving her rape, she shivered against the hard plain of his chest. "It's not the same, Max. I trust you to never do anything to hurt me."

Sean joined them, wrapping one arm around her as he also cupped Max's cheek. "She's right. You'd cut your arm off before you'd hurt either of us."

Anguish clouded Max's dark eyes. "Please tell me you told your folks and that they believed you."

"I did," she said, remembering the look on her parents' faces. They play a prominent role in her nightmares. "My dad was ready to take care of things on his own, but mom talked him out of it." That night she'd been grateful to her mother for stopping him from doing something that would have landed him in jail. Or the morgue. Law and order for the masses of Townsend County was metered out swiftly and severely, if not always justly. "They never considered going to the police since the chief was a cousin to Billy's mother."

"I have a feeling she hasn't told us everything yet," Sean said.

Claire nodded. The worst of her story came after Billy raped her. "In a small town like Maryville you can't sneeze without everyone knowing about it, so I couldn't very well go to the only pharmacy in town to request the Morning After Pill. Three weeks later I discovered I was pregnant."

Claire could still see the blue line on the stick and the look of excitement on her mother's face. "My mother contacted Billy's mother with the good news. My not wanting a baby at that point in my life or the conception being something I hadn't agreed to never factored into her plans. I'd have the baby and in doing so would connect them to the Townsend family and its money."

"Jesus, I don't know who to hate more." Shock colored Sean's words.

She agreed. "I'm still working on forgiving my mom." Her mother's betrayal cut deeper than Claire's physical wounds. She'd been offered up as a sacrificial virgin in order for her family to gain social standing.

When she began telling her story to Max and Sean, she planned to leave off at the rape. She'd use it as the reason why she'd lost the ability to form a lasting relationship with a guy. Now that she'd opened the gate on the truth, there seemed to be no closing it. It didn't make reliving the nightmare any easier. Her scalp prickled with fear as she relived the nightmare.

"After my mother made the call to the Townsends, Billy came over to talk to me. I expected him to deny it was his or offer to pay for an abortion." She remembered the manic look on his face as she stepped onto the wide front porch of her family home. The rest her brother had filled in for her when she awoke several hours later in the hospital. "Instead, he pulled out a knife. It seems he decided the best way to handle the situation was to give me a hysterectomy."

Sean brushed his hand over her stomach. "My God, baby." Emotion made his voice sound like gravel. "How did you keep from bleeding out?"

There were days afterward when she wished she had. "My brother found me. He held his sweatshirt to my stomach till the ambulance could get to me. The doctors operated on me for hours, giving me three pints of blood, but I lost both the fetus and my uterus as well."

"The cops had to get involved after that," Max said. "There's no way in hell your parents could pass that off as consensual."

"The cops did get involved," she said, recalling giving her statement to the police the day after surgery. "Initially. Billy was charged with attempted murder. He spent one night in jail before making bail. Thanks to the lawyer from Mobile the family hired, instead of receiving a prison sentence, he was allowed to plead insanity and was sent to Evergreen Psychiatric Hospital."

Sean tugged her onto his lap. "That's just about the most horrible thing I've heard." He rocked them back and forth, his hold on her tightening. "But I still don't understand why you have to leave if he's in custody."

If the nightmare had stopped there, she'd probably be playing concert piano with some symphony or teaching music to little children in Maryville. Instead, her troubles seemed to grow exponentially. "My story doesn't end with Billy being sent off. His family made sure to tell everyone who'd listen that I'd driven him over the edge. Because their tractor assembly plant was the largest employer in the county, people were afraid to say otherwise."

Claire recalled the few times afterward when she'd come home for visits. "Everyone turned against me. My mother became an outcast to her friends, and my dad was laid off from his job." Then Claire lost her scholarship and had to leave school. That fateful night, when her father called her into the living room was forever etched into her brain. "About three months after Billy was sent away, my daddy sat me down and handed me a check for ten thousand dollars—the contents of his savings account. Then he drove me to the bus station."

"There wasn't one person who'd stand up for you?" Max asked.

The corner of her mouth turned up. "Actually, there was." From an unlikely source considering the strangle hold Billy's family had on Townsend county. "The detective who handled my case met me at the bus station and gave me the business card of an attorney in Memphis, Tennessee who could provide me with a fresh start." One of her greatest regrets was not following through with the change of identity. "I didn't use him back then, and obviously I should have. I contacted him when I got the letter telling me Billy had been released." Claire thumbed over her shoulder to the hall where her things still were. "My new papers are in my backpack."

All the anger had bled from Max's expression, in its place grim determination. "You think Billy's shown up here in Chicago looking for you."

"I'm almost certain of it. I believe he's followed me home on at least two occasions and someone matching his description was asking for me at the store." Guilt twisted in her stomach. "There's something else. I think he may be the one attacking those girls. They match my description, or at least the one in Billy's memory. Young, petite, blonde."

Sean shot Max a pleading look. "Isn't there something you can do?"

Max reached for his phone. "You bet your sweet ass there is. Billy's not playing in his daddy's backyard anymore." He made a phone call to the detective handling the case and relayed Claire's story as well as her suspicions. She held her breath waiting for the detective's disbelief. It never came. Instead, he peppered both her and Max with questions.

Half an hour later, Max wound up the call. "I'll see you in the morning, Detective Price." Then he turned to Claire, his gaze boring into hers from beneath hooded lids. "Part of me still wants to tan your sweet ass for keeping this from me." He tugged her from Sean's lap and banded his arms around her. His heart thudded against her cheek as he held her.

In those precious seconds, their relationship altered from one of lust and secrets to something more. For the first time since she received the letter, she felt as if there was a chance this could have a happy ending. "What does the other part of you want to do?"

"I think I can answer for the both of us," Sean said, adding his arms to Max's.

The three of them stayed like that for a while before crawling under the covers of her bed. The early morning hours ended as they'd begun, with Claire in the middle between two men who were holding onto her as if her life depended on it. Deep in her soul, it felt as if it did. If only there was a way for her to accept Max's help and Sean's comfort without risking their safety.

Chapter Twelve

God, for once Max wished he was wrong about something. His hands shook as he buttoned his uniform. Hours after Claire's revelation, his whole body vibrated with the need to find Billy Townsend and beat the shit out of him. Instead, he was going to make damned sure the law put Claire's rapist behind bars—permanently.

Max tucked his shirt inside his trousers. He was due in Lieutenant Price's office in an hour. When he got there, he planned to talk the lieutenant into bringing him in on the case.

"Have I ever told you that I have a thing for men in uniform?" Claire asked from the doorway of his bedroom. No one wore freshly-fucked hair better than her. Below the tangle of light brown curls, she smiled sleepily at him.

He opened his arms to her as she crossed the room. "No, I don't think you have," he said, nuzzling neck.

Claire yanked on his shirt, trying to untuck it. "Sweetness," he said stilling her hands. "I have to leave in a few minutes."

She ran a lazy hand down the front of his pants, caressing his cock. "I know. I just wanted to leave you with a little reminder of last night."

His hands fisted at his sides when what he most wanted to do was scoop Claire into his arms and tie her to his bed while he hunted down her stalker. "Go snuggle up to Sean. Let him take care of you." His way of keeping her safe wasn't what she needed. Someone who'd been demeaned as she had needed tender love-making, something Sean excelled at.

"He sent me in here to get you." She stood on tiptoe to whisper. "He wants to watch while you spank me again."

He loved seeing Claire's ivory skin turn pink, and remembering her seductive groans as he paddled her behind made him hard. The thought of inflicting pain on Claire now seemed aberrant. "How can you want to have sex with me after what that animal did to you? Especially given the way I fuck."

Smiling as she cupped his cheek, she said, "Remember the first time, when I bolted from the bathroom? I said 'no' and you stopped." She caught his gaze. "You didn't like it or understand what I was doing, but you listened." She kissed him on the cheek. "In that moment, I began falling in love with you."

"That scared you, Claire, didn't it," Sean added, coming into the room. After kissing the top of Claire's head, he came to stand on the other side of Max.

"Still does a little bit," Claire admitted. "But I trust you both."

Trust—a precious commodity for both him and Claire. Maybe they could work toward the three of them building a relationship. If she could trust him after what happened to her, then he certainly could take the step toward building a relationship with her and Sean. His heart ached with the desire to be what both his lovers deserved. First, he needed to keep her safe while he hunted down her stalker.

He tilted her chin. "Speaking of trust, can I trust

you to stay inside today? We talked about this last night. I need to know you're safe."

Claire pulled out of his embrace and crossed her arms over her chest. "I can't stay here, hiding out. I have work and errands to run." She offered him one of her sultry smiles. "If I'm going to be here for Christmas, I want to buy a tree and decorations."

"You don't have to do that," Sean said. "Having you here with us is enough."

"But—"

Max's whole body went cold thinking of her out on the streets. He tilted her chin with a finger, capturing her gaze so there'd be no mistaking how things would play out. "Not. Going. To. Happen."

Anger flashed in Claire's eyes. His little one might like her kink in the bedroom, but that's where the similarities to any sub he'd known ended. "So you'll just tie me to the bed to make me stay?"

"If that's what it takes." Not wanting to fight with her, he offered a suggestion. "I bet I could get Sean to keep you occupied." His buddy could keep her in such a sex fueled haze, leaving the house wouldn't cross her mind.

Claire glanced to Sean then back at Max. "He and I talked while you were in the shower." She rubbed a hand over his chest. "We think it's best if we don't have any one-on-one times, at least for a while."

Sean gripped Max's shoulder. "We're a trio, Max," he said, his hand traveling up to massage Max's nape. "Not a couple with a side of someone else."

Max shoved the memory of David and Lydia to the recesses of his mind. Sean and Claire were nothing like his former lovers. "You'd do that?"

"Anything for you, Max," Claire said.

He nodded, his throat growing thick with emotion. All that stood between him and a future with the two people he loved was making certain Billy Townsend was no longer free to roam it.

"But if you called in sick, Claire, we could decorate the house while Max is at work," Sean said, once again acting the mediator. "Then when Max gets home we can have some together time." He shot Max a heated stare. "I may even let him do to me what he did to you.

A smile curled on Claire's lips. "Could I watch?"

Her eyes hazed with lust. Claire constantly amazed him with her fearlessness, but there were some risks he wouldn't allow her. Max raked his fingers through her hair, pulling her long tresses till her chin tilted. "Only if you promise not to leave the house."

Her eyes widened. "I promise."

"You won't leave for any reason," he added.

Her breath came in shallow pants. "When you come home tonight, Sean and I will be waiting for you."

Max tore his gaze from Claire, checking to see that Sean was okay with them taking things to the next level. His buddy's leer did his talking for him. Max jerked a nod—*okay then.* "If you're good, I'll let you watch while I fuck Sean."

****

Sean locked the front door's deadbolt and rearmed the security system. "It's me, Claire," he called. "You can come out now."

It had taken some convincing, but she agreed to lock herself inside her bedroom while he went out to buy a Christmas tree and decorations to trim it. When she appeared at the top of the stairs, he said, "I got everything on your list."

"You found garland and bows?" She eyed the packages that littered the living room floor.

"And the angel." He held up the tree topper. After finding the perfect tree at the lot up the street from them, he drove to the mall where Claire worked to finish off her list. "I even managed to find icicles. Although I had to ask the clerk what they were." He pointed to the package of metallic strands he suspected they'd be sweeping up well beyond Valentine's Day.

She skipped down the stairs. "This is going to be so much fun. I haven't really celebrated the holidays since I left Alabama."

Sean shared her enthusiasm, especially as she gifted him with a hug for his efforts. His family went all out—as evidenced by his mom's party the night before—making Christmas his favorite holiday.

On the other hand, despite spending the past five years celebrating with Sean's family, Max never embraced the Dalton's love of the holiday. "Don't be surprised if Max has something to say about all these decorations. He isn't crazy about Christmas." When Claire's smile faltered, he explained. "I think it carries some bad memories for him."

Claire stood on tiptoe, kissing him on the cheek. "We'll just have to make new ones."

Sean hauled the tree to the corner of the living room where Claire set the stand. "Yeah," he said, his stomach doing flip-flops. Making love to your best friend for the first time certainly counted as new memories. Sean just hoped he'd be what Max needed in a lover. "Can I ask you something?" he asked after he'd fitted the tree into the stand and made certain it wasn't leaning.

"I like colored lights," she said, holding up the packages he'd bought from the corner drug store. Uncertain what she preferred, he bought both.

"Me, too." He took the strand from her and began winding the lights around the lower branches. "But that wasn't what I wanted to ask you." How did he put into words what he needed to know? He knew the mechanics of making love with another man, but what he wanted to know went beyond Manlovin' 101. "What's it like?" His cheeks heated, not just from the intimate topic he broached but that he was revealing the limitations of his sexual experiences. While he'd seen Max make love to a girl's ass, Sean had never done it. Or had it done to him.

Claire's brow furrowed in confusion before understanding dawned on her face. She laid the box of ornaments she was holding on the coffee table. Then snaking her arms around him she said, "If you're not ready, Max will totally understand."

"I know." Sean found it hard to believe that a week ago he considered himself firmly in the hetero category. Discovering his attraction to Max had been a world tilting revelation. "I want this." Then finding out Max shared the attraction seemed a miracle. Sean wanted to experience with Max what Claire had. That level of intimacy where nothing separated his body from Max's. "Is it like when I'm inside you?" he asked, his hand trailing down to her mound.

"Not exactly, though both feel good when the person doing it knows what he's doing." She winked.

"Trust me, Max knows what he's doing."

"While we're getting really personal, can I ask if you've ever done what the three of us are doing?"

Claire bit her lip. "Before Billy, I had two boyfriends. Neither knew how to do more than missionary. After Billy." She shook her head. "I was too afraid to let anyone see my scars. I didn't want them asking too many questions."

"So how did you know you liked to do what Max likes?" Sean needed to be honest with himself as well as Claire. He liked watching Max dominate Claire, and seeing her ass turn pink had been a real turn-on. Sean wasn't so sure he was ready for Max to do the same to him.

Claire fought the smile playing at her lips. "I read some romance novels that had BDSM as part of the story. The things the people in those books did turned me on, so I bought some toys and tried them out." She smiled at him from a fringe of lashes. "Can I ask *you* a question?"

When she did that, he wanted to give her the world. "Sure."

"When you had other threesomes with Max, did he turn you on?"

"No, not at all," he said quickly. "I mean I liked double penetration, but I didn't want Max to do that to me until you came along." Sean pulled her in close, gratitude making his chest ache. "I guess you revealed a side of me I didn't know existed." Sexual tension hummed between them. He wanted to go down on Claire or maybe fool around a bit until Max got off work and joined them. Instead, he kissed the top of her head and let her go. Their no one-on-one agreement made sense, especially given Max's history.

He and Claire busied themselves trimming the tree and setting out the other decorations he'd bought. They spent the rest of the afternoon cooking lasagna and baking Italian bread they'd share when Max got off work. All the while, lust simmered in his gut.

Nervous excitement shot through Sean's body as the front door opened and closed. He raked a hand through his hair and brushed flour off his jeans. He'd never cared what Max thought about his appearance, and now his feet couldn't get him to the living room fast enough.

Max frowned as he surveyed the room. Besides the tree, Claire decorated the fireplace mantle with three stockings, hung garland over the archway between the living and dining rooms, and set a collection of candles on the coffee table. "It looks like Santa threw up in here."

Claire danced past shopping bags to twine her arms around his waist. "You're home early," she said, pouting prettily. "I wanted everything to be perfect when you got here."

"I could come back later." Max pulled from Claire's hug, but a slow smile formed on his lips.

"No, I'm glad your home." She tugged him back. Claire batted her eyelashes, a technique she'd employed on Sean all day to get him to do her bidding. "I've been very good today."

"Oh, really." Max shot Sean a dark look. "Has she earned her reward, Seany-boy?"

"Absolutely." His voice came out an octave higher than he would have liked. "She didn't give me a bit of trouble."

Desire burned through his nervousness. He craved Max's touch, and closed the space to his lovers in a couple strides. The two men exchanged a single kiss. Then Max's sultry smile turned into a wicked grin, revealing the two men's thoughts were in agreement.

"Ladies first," they said in unison.

With that, Sean scooped Claire into his arms and made for the stairs with Max bringing up the rear.

"My room," Max said, dashing ahead.

Like the three of them rehearsed their actions dozens of times, Max stripped back the comforter while Sean made for the box of condoms and lube from the bedside table. With that done, Sean reached for the top button of his jeans only to become distracted in the best possible way.

Claire shimmied out of her sweats then crawled across the bed. Turning onto her back, she leaned against the pile of pillows Max kept on his bed. Sean's gaze ran the length of her body, from her hair that spilled across her shoulders to the flat plane of her stomach. Seeing the scar that bisected her lower abdomen, he swallowed the bile that burned his throat. He wanted the fucker who'd done that to her put away for good, and envied Max for his ability to play an active role in doing so.

For now, the best he could do was make sure Claire felt safe and wanted. Sean joined her on the bed where he pressed his lips to hers. After a day spent in denial the taste of her kiss was all the sweeter, and not just because of all the peppermints she'd consumed. He wanted forever with her—and with Max if he was willing to take the risk. Sean turned to his best friend who'd shed his clothes and was watching from the far side of the bed. As Max pumped his cock with his fist, Sean said, "I know you like to watch, but taking care of our girl is a two-man job."

"Roger that," he said and arched over Claire.

In doing so, Sean got a good look at his friend's well-muscled back. When Sean gave into the urge and caressed his friend's ass, Max flashed him a grin. "One step at a time."

Sean turned his attention from one glorious sight to another. No wonder Max swung both ways, the sight of Max's masculine shoulders contrasted with Claire's gentle curves made for one erotic ride.

Claire's bare pussy tempted him. He traced a finger over her outer lips. "So beautiful." Then he brought his mouth to the soft skin of her belly where he peppered kisses down to her mound. After nudging his shoulders between her legs, he separated her pussy lips, catching sight of her clitoris. He brought his mouth to the bundle of nerves, teasing it with his tongue.

A muffled groan brought his gaze up Claire's body where Max was feeding her his cock. The sight made his mouth water. *Later.* He redoubled his efforts to bring Claire to orgasm. A girl as open and giving as she deserved to be showered in passion and kept on the verge of orgasm at least twenty hours a day.

Sean inserted two fingers into Claire's hot channel, searching for her g-spot. When he found the raised bump, he worked it with his fingers as he fluttered his tongue over her clit. She rewarded his efforts with a burst of cream that he lapped up greedily. Claire's cunt tightened around his fingers, signaling an impending release.

He hummed against her sex, sending her over the

edge. Sean rode out her orgasm as she bucked her hips. The beautiful sounds she made went straight to his cock. As she recovered, he rested a cheek against the apex of her thighs. The scent of her arousal mixed with the fragrance of her body wash, to fill his head. He could worship her for the rest of his days and not grow tired.

Claire's movement as she sat up brought him out of his thoughts. Her lips were red and plump from sucking Max, and a beautiful flush colored her skin. Her eyelids fluttered open. "You two have proven you're gentlemen." She tugged on his arm, pulling him to the top of the bed. "It's your turn, Sean."

"Are you sure you're ready?" Max asked, brushing a thumb over Sean's cheek.

He leaned into the caress. Knowing Max would use the first hint of doubt as reason to pull away, Sean prayed his voice came out steady. He took a deep breath and opened his heart to his friend. "Make love to me, Max."

Sean thought he might spontaneously combust as Max's calloused hands moved across his skin. His cock hardened to the point of pain while Max eased Sean's jean and boxer briefs down his hips. Then Claire pushed against Sean's shoulders, so that he leaned against the pillows. He brought Claire with him to rest on one side. Then they both watched as Max stalked across the mattress toward them. His shoulder muscles bunched as he crawled up Sean's body.

Sean raised his mouth in silent invitation. He ached for his friend to take him with the same intensity Max showed Claire. When his lips covered Sean's in a tentative kiss, he fisted Max's short hair, fusing their lips.

Max hissed a protest. "Easy." He broke the kiss, and fixed Sean with a dark look.

"You don't have to be gentle with me. This may be my first rodeo, but I'm tougher than I look."

Max let out a breath. "I know, but I don't think I can do that, Sean."

Frustration boiled inside him. "Why not."

Max clenched his jaw, his gaze going from lust hazed to anxious.

Claire cupped Sean's cheek, turning his face toward her. "Because it's you."

Max nodded. "What she said."

"What do I have to do to prove to you that I'm ready for this?" Sean asked, fisting the sheets beneath him.

Max chuckled darkly. "Nothing, buddy. Just promise you'll stop me if I come on too strong."

Still bitter about the be-gentle-with-the-virgin way Max was handling him, Sean growled. "Is this where we have a discussion about safe words?"

"No." Max's gaze darted first to Claire than back to Sean. "No means no. That's all you have to say." He trailed a hand down Sean's body. Then he grasped Sean's dick, giving it a hard pull. The feel of his best friend's hand sent Sean's back arching off the bed.

"Lick the head," he ordered Claire.

Claire scrambled to obey. Her hair covered her face as she drew him into her mouth. As much as he enjoyed looking at Claire's beautiful face it was probably for the best that he couldn't see as she worked his cock with her lips.

Between the delicious things Claire was doing and

Max fondling his balls, it was all too much. When Max's finger slid over Sean's perineum and began to massage his anus, Sean nearly lost it. His head levered up as he sucked in deep breaths and willed himself not to come too soon. Even as their ministrations had him teetering on the edge, Sean craved more. He drew his knees to his chest, giving Max greater access.

"So eager." Max chuckled. Then he reached for the box of condoms and tube of lube. He squirted a small amount on his fingers. "Claire, go easy on him for a bit. Things are going to get intense in a few seconds, and I know Seany-boy doesn't want it to be over too soon."

"Got it," she said, grinning up at Sean from her position at his hips.

Max worked his way between Sean's ass cheeks. Then he pressed a finger to Sean's sphincter. Max circled the ring of muscles before easing a fingertip inside. Sean tensed at the intrusion.

"Relax," Claire crooned.

He did, drawing in a breath as Max pushed his finger inside a little further.

Claire caressed Sean's thigh. "That's it. Now push back against Max's finger."

"Shit, it burns." The words escaped his lips before he could stop them. Max stilled, but Claire stopped him before he could pull back. "That's okay. It's part of the pleasure. Let the burn radiate throughout your body. Feel it settle in your belly."

"God, you're right. That's so fucking good."

Max's finger slid inside past the inner ring of tight muscles. The burning eased as the sensation of fullness took its place. "Feel that?"

"Fuck yeah." Sean groaned.

"That's your prostate. It's going to feel crazy good when I massage it."

Sean gave himself over to the pleasure of Claire's mouth and Max's fingers and barely noted when Max slipped in a second finger. An orgasm boiled inside his nuts and as much as he wanted to prolong the most erotic event of his life, he couldn't. He came with a shout as Max picked up the thrusts inside Sean's ass. Cum shot into Claire's waiting mouth where she drew out every last ounce in greedy pulls.

"Was that okay?" Max asked, his brow furrowed.

All Sean could do was nod. Okay didn't begin to describe the feel of his best friend's fingers penetrating his ass. Max jerked his chin in response and moved off the bed.

"Wait," Sean said, reaching for Max. "This isn't done between us."

The muscles in Max's jaw ticked. Sean held his breath, half expecting Max to bolt from the room or make some smart-ass comment about Sean not being ready. The rejection would kill him. All the tension left Sean's body when Max reached for the box of condoms and began rolling it onto his hard cock. In anxiety's place, nervous excitement knotted in Sean's stomach. Getting fingered felt good, once he got used to the foreign, intrusive feeling. Having Max's thick cock back there was going to take things to a whole other level. One he couldn't wait for. Sean rolled over on his front, propping up on his elbows. Even though he'd just come so hard he'd seen stars, another erection began to stir his cock.

"Don't leave me out." Claire sheathed him with a condom and then slid beneath his body. She arched her hips so that the tip of his cock slid temptingly over her pussy. "While Max fucks you, you can fuck me," she said, giggling.

"I like the way your mind works, sweetness," Max said, his hands kneading Sean's lower back.

As Max's cock nudged at Sean's rosebud, he remembered to relax. Drawing in a breath, he pushed into the cradle of Max's hips. The first intrusion burned and Sean had to grip the pillow underneath Claire's head so as not to cry out for Max to stop. Max stilled, giving Sean time to adjust. Then he reached around to help slide Sean's cock inside Claire as she arched her hips. With the next thrust of Max's hips, Sean slipped deep into her pussy. The twin connections sent all his synapses into overdrive.

"Fuck." Max growled. "So tight." He pushed again, penetrating Sean deeper. "And so hot." Then he pulled nearly all the way out before thrusting again into Sean's ass.

The three of them began moving in a sensual rhythm of thrusts and retreats. Once again, Sean's thoughts turned to the rightness of what the three of them were doing to each other. Claire's whimpers turned to cries as she climaxed beneath him. Her orgasm set off a chain reaction and Sean came again.

While still in the throes of his second orgasm in as many minutes, Max sank his teeth into Sean's shoulder, biting down as Max came in Sean's ass. Afterward, the three of them collapsed into a heap. Their arms and legs tangled with Sean in the middle. Several minutes passed before anyone spoke.

"I'm going to get some washcloths," Max said, leaving for the bathroom.

"Was it what you hoped?" Claire murmured, tugging up the covers and snuggling into his body.

He wrapped an arm around her. "Way more than what I ever imagined," he said, kissing her hair.

When Max returned with several warm, wet washcloths, they cleaned each other daisy-chain style. The last thing Sean remembered before dozing off was the scent of Claire's peppermint body wash and the feel of Max's warm breath against his cheek.

Chapter Thirteen

The next morning, Claire swam up from her orgasm-induced sleep to the sound of deep voices murmuring in the dark. Nestled between two warm, hard bodies, she slept better than she had since receiving the letter a week ago. Perhaps if she was very still, she could return to the lovely dream she'd been having. That proved useless, especially as Max's words filtered through her foggy brain.

"I'll be back around five this evening," he said, his low voice traveling from the other side of the room.

Her stomach knotted. Even before her troubles with Billy resurfaced, she worried about both men getting hurt on the job. Knowing he was actively searching for a man she knew to be crazy with revenge made her nearly sick with anxiety. She'd never forgive herself if something happened to Max because of her.

"Are you good to stay with her?"

Next to her, Sean shifted. "Sure. I swapped with one of the C Shift crew, so I'm not scheduled at the station until tomorrow." He brushed his fingers through her hair, unaware of her eavesdropping.

The mattress dipped as Max sat on the bed. "Good. I don't want Claire left on her own."

She hated being babysat. It wasn't fair to the two of them that they had to rearrange their lives, but they'd extracted a promise from her to let them keep her safe.

Sean chuckled. "That's not going to be a problem." He tucked her closer to his side. "I could easily stay in bed all day." Several beats of silence passed before he asked Max, "Are you okay?"

Claire wished she could see Max's face. Though the three of them had grown closer, especially after last night, he was still the hesitant side to their love triangle. At some point, she would question him about what made him so reluctant when he obviously loved Sean, but now didn't seem the right time. She continued to feign sleep, hoping Max would share the source of his reticence with his best friend.

"Yeah. Why wouldn't I be?" The reply was short, with a bite to it.

"No reason," Sean replied, a touch of humor coloring his words. "In case you were wondering, I'm better than okay."

She cheered inwardly for his deft hand at handling their lover. At the soft sounds of the two guys kissing, she gave up her pretense. "Do I get a goodbye kiss?" She sat up and brushed her hair from her face.

"Absolutely." Max leaned over the bed, drawing her into an embrace. She breathed in the spicy scent of his aftershave as he pressed a kiss to her lips. "See you tonight, sweetness," he said in a low, sensual way that felt more like a promise of decadence than a farewell.

Still, a tendril of anxiety took root when she thought of the dangers he'd face once he stepped outside. Her gaze followed him as he left the room. Helplessness didn't set well with her and she grabbed some clothes off the floor needing to do something other than worry. She padded down the stairs to the kitchen.

God, what a wreck they'd left the kitchen in. Several empty wine bottles lined the counter and the pan of half-eaten lasagna sat in the middle of the table. After the first time the three of them made love, they came downstairs to eat. Then one thing led to another, and they abandoned the dirty dishes and leftovers in favor of round two.

At least cleaning up would give her something to do all day since, at her roommates' insistence, she wouldn't be going into work. She snagged the carafe from the coffee maker and after moving the dirty pots that filled the sink, she set about making coffee for Max to take to work. The two had done so much for her. She wanted to offer something in exchange. Thinking of the way her guys had first made love to her and then to each other reignited desire in her belly.

She was screwing on the cap to Max's thermos when he stepped into the kitchen. Seeing his hair still damp from the shower, she couldn't resist stealing another quick kiss before he left. "I made you coffee along with your lunch," she said, wrapping her arms around his middle. The hard planes of his chest, felt good beneath her cheek. As much as she hated this damsel-in-distress situation, she reveled in the sense of belonging.

"You didn't have to do that," he said, kissing the top of her head. Then he tilted her chin upward, looking her in the eye. "I don't want you thinking that when we're not fucking you silly, you're supposed to be cooking and cleaning for us. You're not our submissive."

Her eyes widened. "I know that," she said, quickly recovering from her surprise. She'd only read about that type of relationship in romance novels. Had he been in that kind of relationship? *Well, duh.* She mentally slapped her forehead. Obviously he had, and going by his furrowed brow, it clearly wasn't something he was interested in repeating. The irresistible urge to pry overcame her. "Can I ask you a question?"

He shrugged. "I guess."

Not exactly an open invitation, but at least it wasn't a door slammed in her face. "Have you ever had a submissive?" Remembering she wasn't the first girl he and Sean shared, she tacked on, "or submissives?"

His jaw ticked. "Yes." He bit out the word as if it cost him dearly to say that much. "A couple."

His answer only added to her questions. "I feel like you and Sean have so much history and I'm playing catch up." She hoped he'd volunteer more. His dark expression snuffed out that hope. She'd hit a nerve as well as a wall—one she'd try scaling at some other time. She brushed her fingers across his freshly shaven cheek. "I was just curious." No better than she liked reliving the dark places of her past, she could hardly fault him for not wanting to either. She also didn't want any of their pasts to shadow what they had now.

The harsh lines of his face smoothed. "I'll see you tonight."

She held onto his hand as he pulled away. "Be safe."

He kissed the tip of her nose as he snagged the thermos from her hand. "Always am."

Claire prayed that was true as she watched him leave. After listening for the sound of his truck as it pulled out of the driveway, she turned her attention to the messy kitchen. Two hours later when Sean came downstairs, her cookie-making assembly line was well underway.

Scrubbing a hand over his head, he asked, "What's all this?"

"I'm baking," she said, brushing flour from her face. She turned to appreciate the delicious way his sweats hung low, revealing the cut line of muscle at his hips she was dying to nibble her way across. However, that would have to wait until Max got home.

A smile playing at his lips, he scanned the room. "For whom? You've made enough cookies to start your own bakery."

"I've got to do something or I'll go nuts." It wasn't only the tricky conversation with Max that had her mind running like a hamster on its wheel, a sense of impending doom lurked darkly in the back of her mind. It kept her from appreciating what she shared with her guys and what she hoped for in the future. She gave voice to her concern, hoping it wouldn't seem so threatening. "I just have this feeling something awful is going to happen. I bake when I'm worried or anxious."

"Do you want some help?" he asked, pouring a mug of coffee.

"No," she said, shaking her head. "It's your day off. Why don't you take it easy?"

"Okay," he said with a shrug. "I'll be in the living room if you change your mind."

Hours later as the sun was setting, Claire snapped the lid closed on the last batch of cookies. Her anxiety had only leveled off despite the marathon baking session. She checked the clock on the stove. Max would be home in less than an hour. Her tummy gave a little flip at the thoughts of the three of them making love like they had the night before. Then when she had him plenty sated, perhaps she and Sean would broach the subject they'd touched on that morning.

****

Sean flew into the kitchen, still tugging his uniform on. Thank God, the fire station was only an eight-minute drive from home. "I got a call from the chief," he said, finding Claire finishing putting baking pans in the dishwasher. "There was a huge pileup on the freeway and they're calling in all the off-duty shifts." Nothing short of a disaster would cause him to abandon his promise to watch over her. The wreck involved a daycare van; he had to go.

She closed the door on the dishwasher, turning the knob to start the machine. "I'll be fine. Max will be home soon."

The rational part of his brain agreed. They didn't know for certain that her rapist was even in Chicago. Still, he hated leaving her, if for no other reason than he made a promise. "You know I wouldn't leave you if it weren't an emergency."

She brushed away his concerns with a smile and the wave of her hand. "Don't worry about me. I'll lock myself in my room if that will make you feel better." After taking off her red and green apron, she headed upstairs with him on her heels.

He pulled back the covers for her as she grabbed her e-reader from the nightstand. "I'll stay right here." She patted the comforter. "Go be a hero."

Staring down at her, worry, love, and gratitude swirled in his chest. He and Max would have never gotten together if it weren't for her. Knowing that, and the realization he was totally in love with her had him

132

wishing he was better at expressing his feelings. He hadn't even used those three little words on her. Nor had he told Max how he felt. Vowing to rectify that as soon as the three of them were together again, he brought her palm to his lips. "Promise me you'll call me or Max if anything makes your nervous." He thought about how busy he'd likely be the rest of his shift. In fact, with Max working, neither one could get to her if the rapist was indeed in town. "On second thought," he amended. "Call nine-one-one."

"I promise." She tilted her chin, giving him an up-close look at her true eye color. Like his favorite season, spring, the blue-green color held a promise.

"We just have to get through this rough patch and then everything will be perfect." Deep in his soul, he knew the three of them were meant to be together. After another kiss, he closed Claire inside her room.

With her holed up safely in her room, he went in full rescue mode. He hoped the injuries on the icy highway weren't serious, even as he mentally prepared for the worst. Ever since he was twelve, he'd wanted to be a fire fighter. His family had been in a car accident and seeing them work a miracle on his sister, Meghan, had cemented Sean's life's ambition.

He raced down the stairs, shrugging on his heavy coat as he hit the back door. The frigid air stole his breath as he paused to lock the deadbolt. He'd taken a couple steps when a blow to the head knocked him against the side of his car. *Son-of-a-bitch!*

Despite the starbursts that stole his vision and the sharp pain that made his stomach heave, Sean knew who his attacker was. The bastard *had* been following Claire. He faced his attacker, just as Billy came at him again. This time Sean was ready, blocking the swing.

He managed to grab the guy by the collar. With short, brown hair and nondescript clothes, the guy could have easily blended into any crowd with his innocuous appearance—as long as a person didn't get a good look into his rage-crazed eyes. "I know the bitch is inside." His voice was a hiss. "You can't stop me from getting to her." Then he broke from Sean's grip, swinging wildly. "She needs to pay."

Sean let fear for Claire's safety and his own anger fuel his defense. They traded blows that left them both winded. If only he could push the fight toward the street, perhaps a pedestrian would see and call the cops. When Billy came at him again, he blocked a swing coming from his right, only to be caught off guard when another made contact with his left temple. It dropped him to his knees.

He took his time getting up, hoping the asshole would come within range. When he did, Sean was ready, tackling the guy and knocking them both against his car. He was able to get in a couple body blows before Billy lashed back, biting his ear. "Fuck," Sean screamed, wiping away the blood that was now running down his neck. This guy was bat-shit crazy and playing for keeps. The rock he now held in his hand proved that. Billy ran headlong at him, and though Sean dodged a direct hit, he couldn't stop the backward motion.

They landed hard on the frozen ground, knocking the wind out of Sean. He gave getting vertical another go. Crawling to his hands and knees, he made it to the other side of the car, where a row of evergreens lined the edge of their yard. Another look into the eyes of crazy and he knew who would win this round. He managed to block a swing to his head, but the boot to the kidneys leveled him. On instinct, he drew his knees to his chest and covered his head with his hands in an attempt to protect his vital organs. Blow after blow came as Billy pummeled Sean with the rock he gripped in his fist.

"I'm going to get at her," he threatened.

As Sean's vision narrowed, he sent up a prayer that Billy wouldn't think to look in his left coat pocket for his keys. After that, rational thought left him, and it was all about warding off the blows. With Billy's dark promises filling his head, darkness overtook him.

****

Max pulled into the driveway behind Sean's car. Something was still off. He'd hoped getting back home would alleviate the anxiety that had been dancing up his spine all day. Leaving the warmth of his truck, he scanned the area around the backdoor for signs of trouble. His hand moved to his service revolver, but neither it nor the lack of any signs of disturbance lessoned the tension. If fact, it only pissed him off that he couldn't get a bead on what was wrong. This was when a couple feet of snow would help, but the bare ground yielded nothing. After looking the length of the house and into the backyard, he let himself inside.

Then he passed through the kitchen, barely noting the sweet scent of cookies still lingering in the air. With his hand still on the butt of his weapon, he scanned the downstairs. Neither of his roommates were anywhere to be found and he mounted the stairs with a growing sense of worry. Hitting the hall, he mentally prepared himself to find Claire and Sean making love. Though they'd made a pledge not to engage in any one-on-one sex, he could completely understand if that proved too difficult a promise to keep. God knows, Max would have a hard time keeping his hands off either one.

The tightening in his gut had nothing to do with romantic worries. The hairs on the back of his neck stood up like they had when he was a kid and his mom brought one of her johns home. Over the years, he learned to listen to that instinct. "Claire, Sean," he called walking down the hall.

"In here," Claire responded, opening the door to her bedroom.

Finding her safe eased some of his tension. "Where's Sean?"

Her brow furrowed. "Didn't you see him on your way out?"

"No." His temper spiked. They'd agreed not to leave Claire alone. Remembering seeing his car in the driveway, Max wondered what kind of errand she'd sent him on. He understood how difficult it was to deny her anything her heart desired, but Sean should have waited.

Claire laid her e-reader down on the bed. "He left just a couple minutes before you got here. You two should have crossed paths," she said, reaching in her closet for her boots. She pulled them on quickly, and then hurried out of the room. "Was his car still in the driveway?"

"It was." Max rushed ahead as adrenaline flooded his system. Why hadn't he taken more time to search outside? He'd sensed something was wrong the second he'd stepped out of his truck. "I'm going to have a look around the house."

"I'm going with you." She reached for her coat.

He snagged her wrist. "The hell you are. You are going to stay right here until I get back."

Anger flashed in her eyes. "I'm not some stupid girl who doesn't know how to look out for herself."

"I didn't say that you were." He took time to caress her cheek so she'd know he wasn't patronizing her. His girl had been smart about her safety. "If something is wrong, I can't have my attention divided between worrying about you and handling the situation."

Her shoulders slumped as she dropped to the little bench in the mudroom. "I don't like it, but you make a good point."

"Thank you," he said, holding her tight for a moment. He didn't know what he'd do if he lost her. With her openness, she made him willing to risk loving again the way Sean's eternal optimism gave him hope for their future. "Go back upstairs until I give you the all clear.

He waited until he heard her bedroom door close before he stepped outside. With his weapon drawn, he dialed Sean's cellphone. The ring echoed in the evening air, and sent Max racing toward the evergreens separating their yard from the neighbors.

"Sean," he called, kneeling down to his best friend's prone body. Max checked for a pulse, and when he found it beating steadily against his fingers, he almost cried with relief. Instead, he called nine-one-one and waited for the ambulance.

Chapter Fourteen

Claire pressed her hand against the hospital room window, feeling the cold seep into her palm. It matched the shards of ice in her chest. *Why? Why? Why?* If only she'd done any one of a dozen things differently, Sean wouldn't be lying in the hospital bed a few feet from her. She glanced at him over her shoulder before turning her gaze back to the view of the lamp-lit street five stories below. The burden of guilt weighed on her until she could no longer look at the bandages that covered his head and face. *Why?*

A gentle hand on her shoulder brought her out of her self-recriminations. "Come take my seat." Mrs. Dalton gestured to one of two plastic chairs. "You've got to be dead on your feet."

Rather than a soothing balm, the woman's tender concern added to Claire's guilt. She blinked away the tears. "I'm fine, but thank you."

With an understanding nod, Olivia left her in peace. The woman crossed the room to her son, smoothing down the hair sticking up from the top of his bandage. After a kiss to his cheek, she moved to stand next to her husband who wrapped a protective arm around her.

In the twelve hours since Max found Sean in the snow, he had been in and out of consciousness. The cracked ribs and bruises to his back and arms would heal with time. At the heart of everyone's worry was the possibility the blow to the back of his head had caused a subdural hematoma. If the doctors detected bleeding into the brain, they might have to operate to relieve the pressure.

At the sound of the door opening, everyone's attention shot to the slender, fifty-something woman wearing a white coat and a reassuring expression. Mr. Dalton was first to ask the question foremost in everyone's mind. "Dr. Chang, is he bleeding?"

She moved to Sean's bedside. "Your son is a very lucky man." She smiled at him and tugged the blanket higher up his chest before turning her attention to the cluster of people in the room. "Though he's sustained a hairline fracture at the back of his skull and a concussion, the MRI shows no sign of intracranial bleeding. We'll want to keep an eye on him, but if all goes well, he can go home in a few days."

With the news that Sean would be okay, Claire let the tears flow. She lost track of the rest of Dr. Chang's conversation, her heart so full of thankfulness that her selfishness hadn't done more damage.

"Oh, thank God." Mr. Dalton shook hands with the doctor. As the door closed on her, Sean's parents and sister clutched each other in a group hug. Lost in thought, Claire hadn't noticed Max had crossed the room until he placed his arm around her shoulder. She shrugged out of his embrace, unwilling to let him comfort her. A pained look crossed his face, which he quickly hid by turning his attention to the monitors surrounding Sean's bed.

Minutes later, the door opened again and a young woman clad in red and green striped scrubs stepped in.

After introducing herself as Sean's dayshift nurse, she went about checking his vital signs. Sean rousted for a moment, muttering something unintelligible.

Mrs. Dalton leapt to his bedside, taking his hand. "Hey, sweetheart. Dr. Chang says you're going to be fine."

He thrashed in the bed for a couple of seconds before falling unconscious. Everyone watched to see if he'd wake and after a few minutes when he didn't, Mr. Dalton said, "I'm going to take Meghan and Livi home for some rest. We'll come back in a few hours."

Claire nodded, relieved. Seeing their pained expressions was nearly more than she could bear. "Max and I'll stay here with him. We'll call if anything changes."

Mr. Dalton squeezed her hand then turned to Max. "When do you have to be back at work?"

"Not for a few days. The captain gave me some time off."

After glancing over at his wife and daughter, he asked, "Any chance you will be able to catch the guy who did this?"

Max's gaze shot to hers. "I'll make sure of it."

"It just makes no sense to me," Mr. Dalton said.

Claire looked over her shoulder at Sean. It made perfect sense to her.

"Unfortunately, the world's a violent place," Max said.

Though guilt tore at her heart, she was grateful to him for not telling Sean's parents she was the reason their son had been beaten and left in the snow to freeze.

After the Daltons left, Max and Claire moved to Sean's bed. They sat shoulder to shoulder, not touching either him or each other. The air between them simmered with unexpressed emotions. Claire bit down on a fingernail, shredding it to the quick. When she tasted blood, she moved on to another finger.

"This isn't your fault," Max said, his voice just loud enough to cover the distance between them.

When he tugged her hand away from her mouth, she jerked it from his grasp. "No. At least not all of it anyway." She met his gaze. "You share part of the blame." Anger and a sense of helplessness burned inside her. "He wouldn't be here if you'd let me go."

He let out a breath then raked his fingers through his hair. "Don't you get it? Running from Billy wasn't the answer. As determined as he is, eventually he'd have tracked you down."

Claire gave voice to what had been in the back of her mind all night. "Maybe I should just let him find me."

He pointed to Sean. "Do you think our boy would want that to be you lying there?"

She bolted, the chair scraping roughly against the tile floor. "I'd trade places in a second if I could." Impotent rage kept her feet in motion.

He caught her by the shoulders. "I know. I would, too, but Sean would give his life for you without a second thought." He brushed back a piece of hair that had come loose from her ponytail. "I would, too, Claire."

She turned her face. "That's what I'm afraid of."

His eyes softened. "You love him, don't you?"

She nodded. "And you, too," she murmured. It suddenly all became too much to bear. This was Billy's retribution, that he would rob her of everyone she let get close to her. "I can't be here."

He cut off her path to the door. "Don't. That asshole could be waiting for you back at the house."

Claire clenched her fist. Another thing her rapist had stolen from her—the sense of security she felt at home. "I won't leave the hospital, but I've got to clear my head. I'll just go down to the cafeteria for some coffee."

She pushed passed him, fleeing the room. Once she'd taken the elevator to the ground floor, she followed the signs to the cafeteria. It was closed for another hour. She couldn't face going back to Sean's room. Not yet. When they moved him from the ER to a private room, she'd seen a meditation garden. If anyone needed to find a little serenity, it was her.

****

Max raked his fingers through his hair when what he wanted to do was put his fist through a wall. He also wanted to chase after Claire. The blame for Sean being in a hospital bed didn't lie with either of them, and he needed to make her see that.

A groan from behind stopped him. "Hey, buddy. It's okay." When the sound of his voice didn't put a halt to the thrashing and gut-wrenching moans, he touched Sean's cheek. "It's all good, my man. Relax." The groans almost sounded like words. He leaned in closer. "What are you trying to tell me? Are you hurting?"

"Claire," came the single garbled word.

What a hero. The guy gets the shit beat out of him, and his only thought is to see their girl was okay. "She's fine, she's fine. You did good." Max tightened his grip on his best friend's hand. "The bastard never got near her." That seemed to work. He let out a long breath and was calm again.

Max reclaimed his seat and watched Sean as he slept. He also gave a little airtime to a plan he had in his back pocket since finding out about Claire's rapist. He'd been clean ever since Mrs. Dalton took him in back when he was a fifteen-year-old with a bad attitude and a juvie record. As a cop, he'd never put a toe wrong. That didn't mean he wouldn't take things into his own hands if need be. First, he needed to get a bead on where the asshole was hiding. After that, he'd get his hands on a gun that couldn't be traced—that's where some of the boys from the old neighborhood would come into play. The bastard didn't know it yet, but his days of terrorizing people were rapidly coming to an end.

He'd been so lost in his thoughts that he lost track of time. Claire should be back soon. His girl was determined to take care of her own problems. Max respected that. Under normal circumstances, he'd stay out of her way. Nothing about this situation was normal. He'd give her another minute then reach out to her. When the sixty seconds ticked past, he pressed Send on the text he'd already typed. *Where'd you go for this coffee, Columbia?*

He trusted her to keep her word not to leave the hospital. Though that didn't mean she wouldn't still try to skip out again once Sean was back home. One thing at a time.

He counted down another minute then hit her up with another text. *I know you blame me for what happened. Come back and we'll talk this out.*

Nothing.

He stood and with his eyes glued to his phone, he

lapped the room.

Three minutes and I'm calling the hospital security.

Those were the longest three minutes of his life. With a backward glance at Sean, he hit the corridor headed for the nurses' station.

Chapter Fifteen

Claire took a few tentative steps into the garden walled-in on all sides by the separate wings of the hospital. With the early-morning sun not yet over the top of the buildings, shadow blanketed the dormant trees and shrubs. The only light came from torches aimed into bare tree branches and a few lanterns lining the brick pathway ringing the space. She paused just outside the pool of light coming from the windowed corridor and drew in gulps of chilled air.

Anger—both at herself as well as Max—still coursed through her. She reined in the recriminations since spinning in circles and assigning blame served no purpose. She slipped onto a bench sheltered by an arbor. *Think!* She needed a plan that would allow her to draw Billy's attention away from Sean and Max but would be clever enough that she could also give him the slip. She concocted then discarded several possibilities that were either too complicated or required cooperation from her lovers. They'd never go along with any scheme that included her leaving. Despite their wishes—or hers—this was what had to be. Waiting for Billy to strike again was no way to live. She didn't need a complex plan or their help. Her original plan would work as long as Billy was still watching for her. Her sixth sense told her he was out there. Waiting.

The decision made, she stood intending to hail a cab at the front of the hospital. As she did, the small sound of a door opening froze her steps. If this was Max, she was in no state to argue with him again. She pulled back into the shadows, hoping not to be noticed. Sure it was a coward's way of handling confrontation, but she didn't have it in her to endure a goodbye.

Rhythmic footfalls against the brick pavers sent shivers across her skin. She held her breath. The steps grew closer, then slowed. "Isn't this a lovely surprise," came a familiar voice from several feet away. "For weeks, I've tried to figure out a way to get you alone and here you just hand the opportunity to me." The casual way Billy spoke, as if talking about the weather or the upcoming holidays, sent shards of fear lancing through her chest the way no obvious threat ever could.

Claire bolted, aiming her steps toward the door. As quickly as she responded, he'd been quicker. Anticipating her path, he blocked her escape. His feral gaze latched onto hers. "Don't make me chase you," he said smoothly. "If you do, I'll only make it hurt more." A sick smile played at his lips. "And you know how much I can make it hurt."

"You're one fucked-up bastard," she said, covering the revulsion she felt.

His grin broadened, growing more sinister. "That's what five years in the state hospital will do to a guy." Closing the distance, he took a tendril of her hair between his fingers.

Bile burned the back of her throat. "You were already like that." She slapped away his hand.

He tilted his head as if considering her retort. "If so, it was girls like you who made me that way." His gaze raked the length of her body. "Teasing me with your tight clothes only to play the virgin when it came time to pay up. You can't play the innocent with me now. I know what a nasty girl you are." He backed them into the darkest corner of the garden. Even if she could outflank him, he'd easily be able to cut off her escape. Her eyes darted to the windowed hospital corridor. In all the time she'd been outside, no one had passed.

A metallic snick redirected her attention. "I'm in a generous mood," he drawled, holding the switchblade for her to see.

She back away until she had no more room to move. Wedged between the two brick walls, she was trapped. Billy inched the blade closer, giving her imagination time to weave a bloody and painful end to their encounter. Finally, he drew the tip of his knife down her neck just breaking the skin. It left a burning trail that made her head swim. "Since you've been so accommodating, I'll make this quick."

She tensed, but made no attempt to run or talk her way out of the situation. What was the use? He'd never stop no matter what anyone did. Resigned to her fate, her shoulders slumped. After years of hiding, they'd come full circle. This time, thanks to pushing Max away, there'd be no help coming. Tears burned her eyes, and then trickled down her cheeks as she waited for him to make good on his promise.

He pressed the knife between her breasts. "Then when I'm done with you." He narrowed his eyes. "I'll take care of your two roomies."

The threat altered everything, flipping her resolution one hundred-eighty degrees. She might not fight for herself, but she'd die keeping him from hurting Sean or Max. And she had but one chance to do that. Her hands darted up, latching onto his knife hand. Before he had time to react, she dug her fingers into the pressure point between his thumb and finger.

He barked out a bitter laugh, and then tightened the hold he had on her nape just as she hoped. While locked in the violent embrace, she shoved her knee hard into his groin. Then she raked her foot down his shin, ending with a stomp to his foot. When he released her and dropped to his knees in pain, she spared a moment to think how proud Max would be that she'd remembered his self-defense lessons.

"Bitch," he screamed between breaths. "I'm going to make you suffer for that."

As he struggled to his feet, she refocused her attention to her next step. If she could find help before he got away, Max would be certain Billy got more than a stay in a mental facility.

She first had to get his knife. It would be too easy for him to send it flying toward her back as she fled. She darted to the edge of the path where it had fallen, but he got there first. They wrestled for a moment, with him overpowering her and knocking her to the ground. He straddled her, raising the knife over his head. Channeling her fear into strength, she gripped his arms and flipped them so that she was on top. Now she needed to knock the switchblade out of reach and incapacitate him enough so she could get help. She managed to redirect the knife away from herself while he writhed and cursed beneath her.

Suddenly he bucked. The knife plunged into his chest with a nauseating crunch as it penetrated through bone. The force of the blow reverberated up her arm, sending a sickening shiver over her skin. Air escaped his lungs in a whoosh and he collapsed against the ground. Horrified, she scrambled off him. The light now peeking over the building tops illuminated his blood darkened shirt and lifeless eyes that stared up at her.

As if he was still chasing her, she fled the garden. Running wildly up the corridor, her only thoughts were to find Max. He'd know what to do. Tears streamed down her cheeks and blurred her vision. She rounded a corner, plowing headlong into someone. Firm hands grasped her. "Let me go!" She fought against the arms that now banded her.

"Claire, what's wrong?" Max's deep voice stopped her.

Relief flooded her and she collapsed against his chest. "Billy," she managed through an emotion-clogged throat. Her nightmare was over.

His gaze darted around the empty hallway. "What? He's here?"

She nodded, letting him tug her several steps back the way he'd come. When she stumbled, he stopped, scanning her with a heated gaze that zeroed in on her neck. "What did he do to you?"

Relief made her giddy and a hysterical laugh bubbled up. "It's what I did to him." Never again would she have to hide, disguise her appearance, or lie about her past.

"What happened?" When she didn't answer right away, he gave her a little shake. "Tell me."

"I killed him." Euphoria and revulsion flooded her in equal measure. She was finally free. But it came at a cost. She'd killed a man. Crazed though he was, Billy was still a human being. Would anyone even believe she'd done it in self-defense?

Max's eyes widened and horror twisted his handsome features for a moment before he hid it behind an impassive mask. "Show me." His low voice came in a growl, and he took her by the hand.

They returned to the garden, to the spot where she'd ended a life. They stood over the body of her rapist. "I had to do it. I couldn't get away." Now she'd have to face the consequences.

He led her to the bench where only a short while before she'd wrestled with how to protect the men she loved. Once seated, she put her head between her knees and drew in a few deep breaths. In all the time she'd wondered how her ordeal would end, never once had she imagined it would be *Billy's* death that set her free.

"Take all the time you need." Max rubbed gentle circles over her back.

She nodded and steeling her nerves let the story pour out. Afterward, Max enveloped her with his arms. "I don't think I've ever been more proud of someone."

"Don't joke." Her gaze darted to the pool of blood a few feet away. "It's not funny."

"I'm not joking." He turned her face away from the body that was turning white as blood seeped out of it. "You took care of yourself when I failed to." He cupped her face. "You fought back and won, baby. Not everyone who does succeeds."

Tears pooled in her eyes again. "Now what do I do?"

His jaw ticked and it was several seconds before he answered. "I have to make the call to Detective Price."

Then he took her hands, enveloping them with his. "I swear it's going to be okay."

****

Still clutching Max's hand, Claire gave her statement to CPD. Her throat raw from tears and responding to the detective's barrage of questions, she took a sip from a water bottle and concluded her statement. "Then I ran out of the garden looking for help, and that's when Max found me."

Detective Price scribbled something on his pad without comment as she braced for another round of queries. Instead, he closed the pad, sticking it in his shirt pocket. "I've heard all I need to, Ms. Mathews. It's pretty clear you acted in self-defense."

Claire clenched her eyelids, relief washing over her.

"Thank you." Her voice sounded worn and reed-thin even to her own ears. Nervous energy had kept her going while she recounted to Max the attack and during the first hour of her interview with the police detective. It burned away during the second hour until now; as he slid back his chair, fatigue nailed her to hers.

As if Max sensed her weariness, he released her hand and helped her up. He hadn't moved from her side during the entire interrogation even when she pleaded with him to check on Sean. She wanted to save him from hearing what had happened. He'd been through enough in the last day, first finding Sean and then her blaming him for their lover's attack. Guilt lanced through her. He deserved so much better than her.

When they reached the hospital's main lobby, he said, "I know you're exhausted, but do you think you can hang in there long enough for Sean to lay eyes on you?" Concern lined his face. "After you left, he was out of his mind with worry over you."

She nodded, tears clogging her throat again. Her men had certainly earned a happily ever after—with each other.

****

The next morning, Claire stepped off the hospital elevator on Sean's floor. While the doctors pronounced him well enough to go home, only Max would have the privilege of caring for their lover. It was time for her to leave. Past time, considering if she left weeks ago, he would have never gotten hurt in the first place. She trailed a suitcase behind her as she walked toward Sean's room. She'd say a quick goodbye then head for the bus station. Though she'd love her two men forever, she'd pretended long enough. The three of them were never meant to be long term.

She rounded the corner past the nurses' station and hearing Max's booming voice, quickened her steps inside. "What are you guys yelling about?" she asked, wondering what he and Sean could have to fight over. "I could hear you all the way down the hall."

Sean stood at the foot of his bed, shoving his shaving kit and clothes into a duffle bag. He refused to look at her, instead continued packing.

Max jabbed a finger at him. "Brilliant here, thinks he's going to go back to his folks' place so you and I can be a couple." His voice grew louder, taking on a desperate quality. "Tell him how crazy you are about him." He gestured between her and Sean. "Make him understand it's *you two* who belong together."

Given her up-close-and-personal experience with real crazy, she wasn't sure it was a word she'd ever use flippantly again. But she was fully and irrationally in love with both men. Even contemplating living without them made pinpricks of anxiety dance along her scalp and an ache set up in her chest. Ultimately, it changed nothing. If ever two people deserved to be together, it was Sean and Max. She swallowed hard past the lump in her throat. "That's what I needed to talk to you both about. I'm leaving from here and heading home to Alabama."

Sean jerked his attention toward her. Pain flashed in his eyes for a moment before he closed the distance between them. Gently, he tugged her further into the room. "That's great, baby." She'd left her hair loose and it fell past her shoulders in waves that he combed with his fingers as he spoke. "I'm sure after all this time, you're anxious to spend the holidays with your folks."

Max came along her other side, studying her as Sean continued stroking her hair. His eyes narrowed. "When will you be back?"

Her courage left her, and as much as she wanted to look them both in the eye and tell them their affair meant nothing, she couldn't do it. Even if she could manage to get the lie past her lips, they'd see the truth in her eyes. Instead, she looked out the window. Huge snowflakes fluttered past on their way to the street below. Tonight her family would probably drive around the neighborhood looking at lights before setting off a few firecrackers at midnight. As much as she missed her family, their country festivities weren't nearly as alluring as spending Christmas Eve tucked between her two lovers, or waking to share presents the next morning. "I'm not."

Max threw his arms up. "What the fuck! Are we just going our separate ways now?" He began pacing the small area between Sean's hospital bed and the bathroom door, swearing under his breath.

When it looked as if he might bolt for the door, Sean cut off his path. "Look," he said catching his friend by the shoulders. "I don't want to go to my parents' house." Then he turned to Claire. "Do you want to leave?"

"Not really." What she wanted was to spend the next several months sandwiched between the two of them and then years after that building a life with them. That kind of thing only happened in the books she downloaded to her e-reader.

Sean turned to Max. "Do you want to be on your own?"

He scrubbed at an invisible spot on the floor with his tip of his shoe. "Wouldn't be my first choice."

Sean rolled his eyes at their lover's attempt at nonchalance. "Good then it's settled. I'll call my mom and tell her I'm going home with you two." When Max opened his mouth, Sean cut him off. "She'll be totally fine with that as long as we all promise to come for Christmas dinner tomorrow," he said, then took the couple steps to sit on the edge of the bed. A mischievous grin curled his full lips upward. "Now then, Claire, you're going to give me twice daily sponge baths, and Max can help me with dressing."

As much as she wanted to play along with his little fantasy, it was time to get real. "So we're just supposed to go back to the way things were before?"

"Sure." Sean shrugged. His smile softened as he caught her gaze. "As much as we can considering what has happened the past two days."

Max crossed his arms over his chest. "What about down the line when you and Claire want to be a couple?"

While he'd stopped pacing and didn't look like he was about to bolt from the room, clearly he wasn't ready to go along with Sean's fantasy. But why did he think she and Sean would ever push him to the side. "I don't follow you." Claire planted a fist on her hip.

Sean shook his head. "Mr. Optimist still thinks he's the third wheel. I keep trying to tell him it's not like that."

Max cut the air with his hand. "Look, I have reason to think the way I do. In the end, this is how things play out." He pointed to Sean. "The hero gets the girl."

Sean's jaw clenched. "I'm no one's hero," he said, regret coloring his words.

Claire took his hand. "That's not true." She wrapped an arm around Max, drawing him closer. "If it weren't for you, I'd still be running from Billy. You two gave me a reason to stay and fight. That makes you the best kind of heroes."

The smile returned to Sean's face. "That settles it then." He stepped over to his bed, shouldering his duffle bag. "You know, the three of us are perfect together. I'm the fun one. Max is the serious one." He cupped her cheek. "And you're the sweet, sexy one." When she rolled her eyes, he added, "The girl filling between two lug-headed beef cakes."

Claire wanted to believe this would work out. She could almost envision them taking turns cooking dinner, watching movies in front of the flat screen, and then all ending up in Max's huge bed where they made love to each other for hours. Max had hit earlier on something. While that arrangement was fine for now, she wanted a relationship down the road that included commitment and a family.

Max gave voice to her thoughts. "So you're saying you want the three of us to be in a long-term, three-way relationship."

"Absolutely," Sean said smiling. "That's exactly what I'm saying."

Max shook his head. "I think he hit his head harder than the doctors thought."

"I'm beginning to agree." Her chest ached. "How would that even work? Do you really think your family would go along with this arrangement?"

Sean considered her words for a moment, then shrugged. "Maybe not at first, but they already love Max, and they'll come to love you, too." He reached for first Max's hand and then drew Claire into his embrace. His playful exuberance settled. "Look, no one outside of the three of us gets a say about how we do this. If it works in your world to fuck men who also happen to be fucking each other, that's all that matters."

Something inside her clicked. Why couldn't she have her fantasy? No one else knew what she'd been through. Nor were there any two people she could better trust with her body as well as her heart. "What do you think, Max?" She finally dared to hope. "Would you be able to trust that Sean and I wouldn't shove you to the side?"

He smiled. "I can, I finally can." Then he brushed back a lock of her hair. "Besides, it'll take two men to love and spoil you the way you deserve."

"We're all yours," Sean added.

Yes, they were. And she was theirs. Forever. "Let's go home. I've got tons to do before Christmas morning."

Epilogue

Christmas Day

Claire slid the quartet of pumpkin pies into the fire station's industrial oven. Warm scents permeated the kitchen and mingled with the cheers and groans drifting in from the nearby day room as Sean's fellow fire fighters watched the Bears-Packers game. Though he wasn't cleared for work, he'd insisted on performing his KP duty—with help from her and Max.

She smiled at her culinary protégé as he prepared a pan of cornbread dressing according to her mother's recipe. Her heart twinged, thinking at this moment her family was doing the same pre-meal tasks. She'd head down to Maryville in a few weeks for Mardi Gras. Sean and Max were her priority now. The three of them were as close and loving as any traditional couple.

Sean caught the other man's gaze, sending him an unspoken message Max rejected with a shake of his head.

At least Claire thought the three of them were in sync emotionally. In the past twenty-four hours, she'd intercepted several whispered conversations and furtive glances.

"Tell me what I'm supposed to do." Max said pointing to a pair of sweet potato casseroles waiting their turn in the oven.

Sean's gaze heated then narrowed. Then he

waggled the huge spoon he'd been using to stir vegetables into the crumbled cornbread. "Oh, the possibilities."

Max barked a laugh. "Don't get any bright ideas, Seany-boy." He turned to include her in the conversation. "The kitchen is the only place either of you gets to boss me around."

"Ask Clair what she wants," Sean said.

She pushed the niggling worry to the corner of her mind. Later, there'd be time to dissect the undercurrent pulsating between her two men. For now, she vowed to enjoy their time together. "You win," Claire said bowing to peer pressure. She gestured to the bag of marshmallows on the counter. Earlier, she and Sean had a mild argument over the appropriate topping for sweet potato soufflé. "You can put those plastic pillows on top if you like."

A piercing bell interrupted her lover's victory dance followed by the station's three-tone signal. "Station 11, Engine 5, house fire in progress," the dispatcher said followed by the address.

The crew, despite offering to help with food prep had been shooed into the day room. They now erupted into a scurry of well-practiced action, spilling into the kitchen on their way to their respective trucks. Beside her, Sean tensed. His eyes followed his team as they raced to the bay. The bay's great doors trundled up, engines roared to life, and sirens blared. Then the only sound was the T.V. still playing in the other room.

"Couple more weeks," Max said, gripping his shoulder.

Guilt pierced Claire's chest. Her past nearly cost Sean his life. If she lived to be a hundred, she'd never forget the sight of him in that hospital bed, or forgive herself for putting her lovers in danger.

"You go watch the game. I can finish up in here."

Sean opened his mouth to object, but Max intervened. "Come on," he said tugging on Sean's arm. "Remember what the doc said about over doing it."

Claire sent Max an appreciative smile. He seemed to understand her need to pamper their lover. After the two had settled into the other room, she turned the burner down on the green beans cooking on the stovetop and peeked in on the pies. She eyed the clock and did some mental calculations. Going by the other calls that morning, the crew would be out at least an hour. It seemed all of Chicago decided to brave the frigid temperatures and deep-fry the family's Christmas turkey. The result kept the fire fighters busy extinguishing deep fryers placed too close to the house.

Max settled his arm around Sean's shoulders and the two embraced lazily on the sofa in a display of affection they couldn't afford with an audience. The sight stirred a simmering lust in her belly. Since leaving the hospital, there'd been no sexy times in deference to Sean's injuries. He might not be up to more rigorous lovemaking, but there were less strenuous activities they could indulge in.

Claire padded to the day room, rounding the sofa to stand in front of her men. She dropped to her knees and nudged her shoulders between the tangle of legs. Her pulse raced as she reached for Sean's zipper.

"Whoa, wait. The crew could be back any minute."

Max chuckled darkly. "If you're as horny as me, that's about all it's going to take."

Sean laughed as he shoved his jeans down his hips.

Claire brought her lips to his waiting cock, sucking him to the back of her throat while Max offered naughty encouragement. As predicted, Sean shot off after only a few strokes of her tongue. While he recovered, she made a move for Max. He too stilled her hand as she made for his zipper.

"No way, sweetness, it's your turn," he said, making room for her on the sofa.

"But I only wanted—"

Her men didn't let her get out the rest of her protest, and by the time they had her skirt shoved up to her hips and her panties pushed to the side, she couldn't think straight much less explain she'd only wanted to give them the release they needed. If anyone was keeping track, moments later she set the record for shortest sprint to a climax. Which was a good thing as the rumble of trucks began filling the air.

"Tough luck, buddy," Sean teased as he gripped the front of Max's jeans. He moaned good-naturedly as the three of them rearranged their clothes and moved back to the kitchen.

The next hour rushed by, with all hands on deck as they pulled the meal together. Even as Claire relished the meal that reminded her so much of home and accepted praise from the fire fighters, she couldn't settle the disquiet in her chest. She meant the seduction in the day room as a substitute for the words she didn't yet have the courage to say. As Max and Sean resumed their non-verbal communication, she worried if it was enough.

Finally after the meal had been eaten and the kitchen cleaned, she slipped outside to collect her thoughts. Should she voice her worries, or ignore the tension arching between her lovers? She breathed in the cold air, hoping it would clear her mind. The soft snick of the kitchen door pulled her thoughts to the present.

"The boys are still raving over your turkey." Sean slipped behind her to engulf her in his embrace.

"It was all you." She leaned her head into his chest. "You know you're never getting off kitchen duty."

He shrugged. "Could be worse."

"What are you two doing out here?" Max joined them on the small patio that separated the firehouse from the parking lot.

"Just taking a break. I think it's going to snow tonight," she said, feigning a nonchalance she didn't feel—especially as from the corner of her eyes, she caught the pointed stare Sean shot Max.

When they'd committed to their ménage relationship, a key piece of their relationship puzzle had been missing. More specifically a key declaration was missing. She screwed up the courage to share her feelings. She wiggled out of Sean's embrace so she could face both her men.

"I've been trying to find the best time to tell you guys this." Claire's heart pumped hard against her chest.

Max's eyes narrowed. "Just spit it out."

Sean swatted the other man. "Give her a minute." Then he turned to her. "If you want to spend time with your folks, we'll understand."

"That's not it." What if it was too soon? Or worse, they didn't feel the same. Maybe those looks they'd been giving each other were because they wanted to break up. Her emotions bubbled to the surface and tears stung her eyes.

"I love you." She let out a breath. "There, I said it. I understand if you two don't feel the same way. I just needed you to know."

They were on her before she could think, hugging her from each side. "Is that what had you worried, sweetness?"

Sean beamed. "We love you, too."

Max brushed the back of his hand down her cheek. "What he said."

Claire stood on tiptoe to kiss both men. "You really don't have to say it back."

"If you haven't noticed, he didn't." Sean pointed an accusing finger at the other man.

A pained look washed over Max. "I love you." He bit the words out. Then he turned his gaze on Sean. "You, too, Seany-boy. I love you both. Satisfied?"

"Absolutely," she said, knowing how difficult it was for him to put his emotions into words. Her hope that with the declaration they'd settled things once and for all was quickly squelched when Sean shot Max another one of his glares.

"I thought we were going to wait until we got home," Max said.

"She needs it now."

"Impatient much?"

"Says the guy who wanted to slip off to the bunk room for his turn."

All Claire could do was watch the conversation between her lovers and hope at some point they bothered to clue her in. Finally, Max shrugged and fished out a small box from inside his jacket. He placed it into her waiting palm with a hand that shook despite his seemingly indifferent behavior.

"Are you sure?" she asked.

"Of course," Sean said.

She waited for Max's nod then pried open the lid. Nestled in black velvet, a ring of three silver loops sparkled in the outdoor security light.

"Max thought you might want us to give you a diamond."

Her hand shook as she slipped the interlocking circles onto the third finger of her left hand. "This is perfect."

Something seemed to settle in Max. He gathered them into an embrace and let out a contented sigh. "My thoughts exactly."

Large flakes begin drifting down. She closed her eyes and tilted her face to the sky, and thanked the stars that she was theirs.

About the Author

Melissa Klein writes sexy contemporary romances about everyday heroes fighting extraordinary battles. Whether facing the demands of caring for a child with special needs or the struggles of a soldier returning home, her characters take on the challenges life throws at them with perseverance, courage, and humor. Her characters will have readers rethinking the definition of hero, what it means to be sexually attractive, and who deserves a happy ending.

~*~

Visit Melissa at

http://www.melissakleinromance.com

~*~

To chat with Melissa Klein and other Wild Rose Press authors of erotic romance, join us at

www.groups.yahoo.com/group/thewilderroses.

Also Available

Double Her Risk

Boston's Brave

By Samantha Cayto

https://amzn.com/B00O5VPKL4

After the deaths of his parents and having to raise his younger brother, Detective Ronan Callaghan looks for three things—a good time, his next case, and when time allows, the man who murdered his family. The jury is still out on his new partner, but the hot new medical examiner at the first crime scene they share does it for him hands down.

Diego Nieves hopes his new job in Boston will allow him to shake the painful memories of an on-duty shooting. Haunted by the event, he takes his job seriously and isn't certain he can work with a cavalier partner. He sure as hell wants to work more closely with the pretty ME standing over his first homicide vic.

Newly free from a long and boring engagement, medical examiner Cassidy Barnes is finally free to cut loose with her sex life. She's determined to break old patterns and start taking new chances. When two sexy cops catch her eye, she can't resist either—the charming rogue or the serious romantic.

Just when Ronan and Diego begin to click as partners, their simultaneous relationship with Cassidy pits them as rivals. As each man vies for her attention, Cassidy struggles to choose between them. Solving the case and keeping Cassidy just might mean Ronan and Diego must to learn to work together…in more ways than one.

Also Read
Bound & Teased
By Marie Tuhart
https://amzn.com/B01358LYQM

Eight years ago, a naive Katie Crane ran from Ry and Jed, warned their brand of love would ruin her life. Now she's all grown up and returning home with a better understanding of the BDSM lifestyle. After the betrayal she's faced at her father's hands, she worries she won't be strong enough to submit to the men she gave her heart and virginity to at eighteen.

Jed Malloy and Ry McKade are surprised and thrilled by Katie's return to Felton's Creek. They'd been heartbroken after her departure and had turned to each other, embracing the BDSM lifestyle without her. Katie's homecoming sparks hope and worry. Ry isn't sure he can keep his dominant side under control, and Jed fears Katie will see him as less of a man by being a switch and Ry's submissive.

Having Katie back could mean the beginning of everything they've ever wanted or the end to the only family they've ever known.

Thank you for purchasing this
publication of The Wild Rose Press, Inc.
If you enjoyed the story, we would appreciate
your letting others know by leaving a review.
For other wonderful stories, please visit our
on-line bookstore at www.wilderroses.com.

For questions or more
information contact us at
info@thewildrosepress.com.

The Wild Rose Press, Inc.
www.thewilderroses.com

Stay current with The Wild Rose Press, Inc.
Like us on Facebook
https://www.facebook.com/TheWildRosePress
And Follow us on Twitter
https://twitter.com/WildRosePress